Our Circus Presents . . .

Originally published in Romanian as *Circul nostru vă prezintă:* by Editura POLIROM, 2002
Copyright © Lucian Dan Teodorovici, 2002
Translation copyright © Alistair Ian Blyth, 2009
First English translation, 2009

Library of Congress Cataloging-in-Publication Data

Teodorovici, Lucian Dan, 1975-
 [Circul nostru va prezinta. English]
 Our circus presents... / by Lucian Dan Teodorovici ; translated by
Alistair Ian Blyth.
    p. cm.
 "Originally published in Romanian as Circul nostru va prezinta... :
by Editura POLIROM, 2002"--T.p. verso.
 ISBN 978-1-56478-556-5 (pbk. : alk. paper)
 I. Blyth, Alistair Ian. II. Title.
 PC840.43.E15C5713 2009
 859'.335--dc22
                    2009026557

Partially funded by a grant from the Illinois Arts Council, a state agency, and by the
University of Illinois at Urbana-Champaign

Partially funded by the Translation and Publication Support Program of the
Romanian Cultural Institute

www.dalkeyarchive.com

Cover: design and composition by Danielle Dutton, illustration by Nicholas Motte
Printed on permanent/durable acid-free paper and bound in the United States of America

Lucian Dan Teodorovici
Our Circus Presents . . .

translated by Alistair Ian Blyth

Dalkey Archive Press
Champaign and London

to my mother, Lucica, and to my grandfather, Florea, who are no longer among the circus spectators

Chapter One

This is the position in which I start the day today: mouth open, cheeks puffed out because of the rush of wind—like in the train, when you stick your head out of the window and, grimacing into the blast of air, you turn your buccal cavity into a balloon—chin at an angle of one hundred and twenty degrees to my throat, arms splayed wide, legs bare, trembling, the soles of my feet glued to the cold ledge of a fifth-floor window.

Just as on every other day, I want to commit suicide. It's morning, the sunrise is for the time being swathed in clouds, and there are no passersby, so I can still permit myself to want to commit suicide. In any case, the whole business, which I have been repeating for such a long time, I can't even remember since when, will probably last another five or ten minutes. After which I'll either go back inside, or I'll . . . "Either," my ass! I've spent too many mornings waiting for a suicidal urge, freezing like an idiot on this window ledge, to go on believing it might still come. Something else will happen. Soon, someone—a passer-by under my window—will notice me. After which, out of excessive concern for me, he'll shout: "Hey you! You nut! What the hell are you trying to do, kill yourself?" Or he'll irritate me: "Mister, it's no good killing yourself." And I, as is my wont, will go back inside, afflicted by a certain feeling of shame, I'll start cursing at my lack of courage and, above all, at that urge which refuses to come. Then I will . . .

"Hey you, what are you trying to do down there? Kill yourself?"

This time, strangely enough, the voice comes from somewhere overhead. I look up and, on the seventh floor, maybe the eighth, I can't really tell, I see a bearded man with glasses (someone who's recently moved here, or else the boyfriend of some neighbor) shaking a lit cigarette at me.

"What the hell are you fooling around at?"

"Nothing," I reply, attempting an innocent smile.

"What do you take me for? An idiot? You're telling me that you're standing there, hunched over on the ledge, and you're not up to anything?"

The man is yelling at me from the seventh floor, as is clear to me now. Two windows higher . . .

"But what do you want me to do?"

It's clear that he's confused by the question. He hesitates for a few seconds, before resuming the dialogue.

"Well . . . I don't know," he says at last. "How the hell should I know?"

"Well then, if you don't know, why do you expect me to do something?"

"Because you're standing there, at the window, as if you wanted . . ."

He loses his temper:

"What do you take me for? Some kind of idiot? I'm sure you were intending to commit suicide, damn it! Don't try to tell me that that wasn't your intention!"

"Not true!" I shake my head determinedly. "Does it look to you like I'm crazy? I came out to take a breath of fresh air."

Although the distance between us is quite great, I can see his eyes boggling, then I notice how he makes the sign of the cross with the hand in which he's holding the cigarette.

"On the window ledge? In your underpants?"

"Precisely," I say. "Do you think that I would commit suicide like this? What normal person would commit suicide wearing only his underpants?"

"Don't try to explain, I've seen other nutcases like you! So what if you're in your underpants, does that mean you can't . . . ?"

He breaks off his shouting and gesticulating, as though he has just been struck by a revelation. Then—probably as a result of that revelation—all of a sudden he spits at me. Miffed at not hitting his target, he doesn't stop there. The next instant, just as unexpectedly, he furiously flings his cigarette at the ledge where I'm standing. I manage to dodge it at the last moment. And, losing my balance, I barely manage to grab hold of the window frame, thereby saving myself from an unwanted fall, unwanted inasmuch as it wouldn't have been due to the urge I've been feeling for so long. Before I get a chance to swear at him, he does so:

"Fuck you! Look at what I'm talking to! Go on then, kill yourself, you nut! Nobody said I had to look after you! One fewer idiot in the world . . ."

"I'd be grateful if you fucked . . . I mean, fuck you!" I shout back, realizing in time that I had started out a wee too politely for an effective obscenity.

The man overhead waves his hand, as if to say: "I'm not going to get sick over some idiot who's thinking of committing suicide at the exact moment I decide to look out of the window." He mutters something else, and then vanishes back inside. Because there's no more point in me standing here and, above all, because I'm starting to feel a chill, I go back inside as well.

On this occasion, the dialogue with the man who stepped in to save me was longer than usual. Moreover, in order to find suitable answers to his irritated questions, I had had to put my spontaneity somewhat to the test.

I slump in the armchair and start to laugh. There's nothing else for me to do, given that I'm fully aware of how ridiculous my attempts to leave this world are. In fact, I think I'm the only one who's aware of just how ridiculous. The people who see me with my arms opened wide, on the ledge of my window, more often than not take the situation very seriously. Some of them, pedestrians passing my block of flats below, even start talking to me from down there, about various reasons to be happy, about the life which, in spite of countless inconveniences, is still worth living:

"Yes," some admit sagely, "yes, life is like a bad cake base. It crumbles when you least expect, it breaks in two, pieces of it go to hell. But what about the icing? What about the syrup? If you know how to coat the base in syrup, if you know how to add the right filling, in the end you'll have a delicious cake. With a bad base, granted, but still delicious . . ."

Others, out of a desire to be as convincing as possible, don't hesitate to give me their own examples:

"My dear man," says the person in question and looks anxiously left and right to assure himself that no one apart from me is listening, "my wife cheats on me at every opportunity she gets! I'm sent out of town on business . . . What does she do? She cheats on me! I'm admitted to hospital . . . she cheats on me, because she can't wait for me to get better, oh no! I'm at a party with my friends, so she—it goes without saying—cheats on me. But so what, does it mean I have to suffer so much that I end up killing myself? Better to give her a couple of slaps, I cool off and . . . That's my philosophy!"

Every time one of them gives me a talking to, I go back inside, giving him a broad, grateful wave, thereby offering him the satisfaction of believing that he's saved me. From behind the curtain I watch him go on his way. Then I imagine him, at work, telling his co-workers about his brave act. And I am content. "Look," I often happily think to myself, "if my suicidal urge still has no intention of coming to fruition, at least I have the satisfaction of being able to offer a man the unique chance of saving someone else from death." Yes, I must admit, that is one of the few pure joys in my life . . .

But today I was unable to offer myself even this joy. Today all I managed to do was annoy the person who intervened to save me. And so I can't imagine him recounting his brave deed to anyone . . . Because of this, the only thing left is for me to be bored.

I don't know why, but when I was little—it happened a long, long time ago—my father deemed it fitting to tell me a story, an anecdote, a joke—yes, I think he told me it in the form of a joke—about a circus. So, a circus comes to town (I don't remember which town), and the poster looked something like this:

THE MAIN ATTRACTION!
OUR CIRCUS PRESENTS A UNIQUE ACT:
THE BIRDMAN!
ONE DAY HE FLIES, THE NEXT DAY HE DOESN'T.
HE'S NOT FLYING TODAY!

I've no idea how my father thought I could get the joke. What is certain is that, at the time, only he laughed at the punch line. I looked at him as though he were a stale comedian, I slapped a complaisant smile on my child's face—at least that's what I think I did—and I went on playing. Except that from that moment on my father, every time something wasn't quite right in his opinion, would remind me of that wonderful parable. If I didn't want to do my homework, giving him a "later" that concealed an inclination to play, my father would smilingly admonish with upraised finger:

"The birdman, eh? He's not flying today!"

If I was late taking out the garbage, I used to see the same raised finger and hear:

"Not flying today, is that it?"

I didn't get the meaning of this joke, anecdote or whatever it may have been until I was about sixteen or seventeen. I can say that it was the first major revelation in my life. I had been going out with a girl for about two years. As far as I remember, my father, a man whose behavior was absolutely lacking in any inhibitions, got it into his head to talk to me about sex. As sex at that time was a mystery to me, I listened to him for half an hour with a fascination that I had the good sense to disguise beneath an embarrassed face. And at the end of that manly talk, my father asked me a most indiscreet question for my age:

"Tell me," I heard, "do you have sex with your girlfriend?"

Probed in the hidden crannies of my carnal desires, blushing, embarrassed, I nonetheless managed to give a timid answer, after a few good seconds of hesitation:

"Not yet."

Then, realizing that my manhood had been cast into doubt by the adult before me, I added, trying to seem more sure of myself:

"But it hasn't been time wasted. She's given me her word of honor that we'll do it soon!"

I feel like laughing when I remember it. Just as my father felt like laughing when he heard it. And, amid his guffaws, he said:

"The birdman, eh? Today he's not flying!"

I must admit that, getting the joke, anecdote or parable at last, I was so strongly affected by its meaning that the very same day, taking advantage of the fact that she was home alone, I impetuously demanded that my girlfriend should undress so that we could have sex. She, just as impetuously, slapped me twice and threw me out.

It's not toward her, toward that girlfriend, that my memory now turns, however. But rather toward that moment of revelation. Which, for me, was the start of accounting for any incapacity in terms of the joke once told by my father.

And so it is now. Now, as I sit in the armchair looking at the window ledge I have so often felt beneath my bare soles, I repeat, amid stupid guffaws of laughter, that, almost naturally, the Birdman is not flying today either.

∾

This is how my day, which began with me waiting on the window ledge, continues: I'm sitting slumped in an armchair. With the remote in my hand. With the television six feet away. With the boredom of snore-inducing politicians' speeches. With the alternative of Daffy Duck. Or Elmer Fudd. With fuck-knows-what-else every five, ten, fifteen minutes. Whatever the fancy strikes me.

I'm going out of my mind with boredom.

I'd like the telephone to ring today, although it's hard to believe that anything like that will happen. Too few people know my number. Not that I wouldn't want lots of people to know it. As far as I'm concerned, if I thought there was any point to it, I'd paste my number on every fence post. But there aren't many people around me who would be interested in that number. Because of that I'm now obliged to listen to a long-winded psychologist advocating ideals: "Ideals are the motor of mankind. Of course, they can't be attained by the vast majority of people, but idealists, esteemed viewers, are, as shown by research carried out by experts, the main candidates for success in life.

That's because an idealist, although he's almost certain that he will never reach the stage where all his wishes are fulfilled, will, by following his dream, definitely achieve at least a part of what he has set out to do . . ." And so on. Superb. Hope-inducing . . .

My ideal is to invent a gadget, a kind of magnet, which will somehow attract all the loose change lost by people all over the world. To attract it into my flat. I don't want to steal it. My ideal is a noble one. I'm content merely to salvage, in my own home, all the loose change people lose in—let's say—the course of a month. Anyhow, once that money is lost, it's no longer of any use to those it formerly belonged to. Why shouldn't I make use of it? Here is an ideal worthy of an honorable idealist, which is how I think of myself. According to the words of the windbag on TV, I'll never achieve my dream. Sad. But, according to the words of the windbag, I have every chance . . . in fact no—I'm convinced that, in part, my dream will be fulfilled. Which would somehow mean, according to the view of the psychologist, that I'll soon be rich. Yes, I admit, I'll never collect all the loose change lost by all the people in the world. I'll have to be content with just the change lost in one month by Americans, Germans, and Frenchmen.

Can boredom lead to madness?

From the porno magazine I keep on the coffee table, a number of high-class sluts flash pearly-white teeth at me, urging me to step into the bath with them. Nothing could stop me from whiling away a few minutes with them. But even that pastime has become boring. Because, ultimately, anything, no matter how satisfying it proves to be in its initial phase, ends up becoming insipid if repeated too often. Then again, there's something else that prevents me from succumbing to the temptations of the sluts in the magazine: since my neighbor caught me in the act, I've felt a certain embarrassment.

My neighbor—who out of the goodness of her heart offered to tidy up my flat whenever I deemed it necessary—made use of the key I had provided her with, entering on a day when she thought I was out. Usually, when she knew I was in, she would knock on the door. I don't know what it was that I'd arranged to do, but I had given her to understand that I would be away for a couple of days. I had intended to leave, but then I changed my mind, I don't exactly remember why. What is certain, however, is that I forgot to inform my neighbor of my sudden change of plan. And so it was that she, as well-meaning as ever, who made use of the key, entered with a broom in one hand and a dustpan in the other, and . . .

How easily things that were stupid and degrading at the moment they occurred become acceptable once transformed into memories!

Again I laugh. Nonetheless, this time with a certain embarrassment. There I was, naked, stretched out in the same armchair in which I'm now sitting, with a porno magazine in my hand . . . There she was, the neighbor, rooted to the spot. There I was, also rooted to the spot, but rooted to the spot in a posture which only with an effort of dignity I might name merely indecent. There she was, the broom falling from one hand, the dustpan falling from the other with a clatter onto the floor. There I was, swiftly covering up my genitals with both hands.

"Hello," she eventually saw fit to greet me. "I thought you were away."

She uttered those words staring fixedly at my hands, which were, still in vain, trying to cover that spot.

"I should have been," I stammered. "But . . . what can I say . . . I was just about to have a bath . . ."

"Yes . . . Well . . . I think it would have been more appropriate in the bathroom, to do what you were . . . In general, it's in the bathroom that people do that sort of . . . But not to worry, I understand . . ."

Words that concealed other thoughts. Stammering. In my case, born of the inability to justify myself. In her case, the fruit of her striving to accept the situation, without any kind of justification on my part.

And nevertheless, I had to explain myself somehow.

"No, madam!" I answered firmly. Then: "I think that . . . you have somehow taken things the wrong way. I got undressed because I wanted to take a bath. To get washed, that is. To get into the bathtub, if that makes it any clearer."

"What about that magazine?"

I had forgotten about the magazine, and at her question I felt the need to toss it as far away as I could. And toss it I did.

"Well . . . that . . . it just came into my hands . . . I don't know how."

A sparkling answer. As though the magazine had dropped from the ceiling or somewhere. She nodded, serious, understanding, well-meaning. And I, in the ludicrous position that I was, instead of thrusting my head between the cushions, like an ostrich, I found myself suddenly noticing that, all the time we had known each other, I had never seen her laugh.

"Don't worry," she said, as if the situation were nothing out of the ordinary. "You don't have to explain. There's no need to be embarrassed."

Those words, uttered with such seriousness, weren't far from seeming an invitation to continue what I'd been doing in her presence.

"My husband, God forgive him, used to do it now and then . . ." she added, pointing at the area I was hiding. "While I was pregnant. You realize we couldn't make love after I was pregnant. So he had to . . ."

"Yes you could have." I felt obliged to enlighten her. "You could have. It's only in the final month that it's not recommended."

My neighbor looked at me in astonishment.

"Is that right? I could have made love to him? How did you know that?"

"From the magazine I've just tossed away, and others of its kind," I ought to have told her. There are psychologists everywhere, not just on television. Television psychologists either solve grave family problems or teach us how to be optimists. The ones in salacious magazines help girls to cope with their first period, to reassure female readers who have a problem with the length of their partner's member, and even inform said partners that it's not the length that matters, but rather, according to the case, the angle of penetration, the science of finding the G-spot, or, naturally, thickness. Useful things, of course, except that I sometimes think that I'm the only reader of these useful things—at a given moment, boredom causes me not to be aroused by the glossy pictures, but to read all the articles, all the stupidities trapped between the covers of that kind of magazine.

And the same boredom gives me sufficient time to think that I'm the only reader, or, in any case, among the few readers of those texts. Who buys a pornographic magazine in order to read it?

"From the medical almanac," I answered the woman.

"Is that right!" my neighbor repeated, with visible regret. "And when I think that he, the poor man . . ."

The conversation had become a normal one, I had already got used to the situation, so much so that it didn't enter my head to put on a dressing gown. And it seems that she had got quite used to it too, given that she bent down, picked up the broom and dustpan, and then addressed me, with a sigh:

"It's pointless me finding out now. My husband's dead, as you know."

"Maybe you should remarry."

"Hell no! Who would marry me now, the way I look? I'm almost fifty. And then," she whispered, "I'm already in the . . . what do you call it? When you can no longer have children?"

"Menopause?"

"Aha."

And the conversation continued for a good few minutes, maybe even an hour, along the same lines. And as a result of it . . . That situation drew my neighbor and me closer together, probably it drew us closer together than would otherwise have been the case. In other words, from that moment on, she no longer came into my flat just to do the cleaning.

In time, however, my neighbor moved out of town. She inherited a plot of land, somewhere about fifty miles away. And, even if she had wept bitterly at the separation, in the end she left.

And I was left with only a few memories of her, with the image of a woman who almost never laughed, regardless of the situation, and with the lasting embarrassment of having been caught doing what she caught me doing. But that's enough memories for today!

And that's enough porno magazines! It's obvious they don't do me any good; ultimately, I'm still young, I'm just thirty-two. Can't I find a more honorable way of spending the day? I have to get the hell out of the house . . .

Chapter Two

And so nothing else remains for me to do except get the hell out of the house, breathe the clean outside air, lose myself among the inhabitants of the city, and hope that I'll run into some friend, some acquaintance, or witness some event, something. Something!

At the tram stop, impatience is playing tricks on me. I think I recognize an old girlfriend, I draw closer, I tap her lightly on the shoulder, then I squat down so that when she turns her head she won't see anyone, won't know who has touched her. The girl, naturally, lets out a scream when she sees me crouching at her legs. I look up at her from down below, gaily waving one hand in the air, my mouth grinning as if to say: "See what a clever practical joke I've played on you?"

And, before I can wipe the kindly smile off my face, I hear:

"What's wrong with you? Are you an imbecile or what?"

Maybe I *am* an imbecile. But if that were the truth concerning me, I certainly wouldn't admit it to a person who is a complete stranger to me. And so nothing else remains for me to do except quickly stand up and apologize, in embarrassment:

"I mistook you for someone else, sorry."

She grimaces, visibly bored by such banal masculine wiles. She grimaces as expressively as can be, in profound disgust and withering scorn.

"These idiots," I hear her muttering as she moves away, "all hitting on me, as if I'd look twice at such a . . ."

"I did mistake you for someone else, you know!" I shout, irritated at the insinuation directed at me.

I desire relationships with women, it's true. I even desire them desperately. But it's a calm desperation, one that unfolds within the limits of propriety. My desperation doesn't go so far as to compel me to attempt such ludicrous pick-up procedures. I do have a certain pride!

"To hell with her," I whisper to myself before boarding the tram. Then, having boarded, I look all around me, smiling in preparation, ready to greet any eventual acquaintance. As all the faces I scrutinize are completely unknown to me, a minute later I sit down, disappointed.

At the next stop, as I fix my eyes on the window, trying to spot some familiar person in the crowd or to be witness to some occurrence with an aura of being an event, some gypsies get on, coming to a halt right next to my seat.

Although I probably ought not to let myself be carried away by their appearance, my mind persists in unfurling a play of thoughts, in which, inspired by my neighbors in the tram, it starts to outline the faces of some women with flowery skirts who are washing clothes on a riverbank, singing songs in their own language. My imagination sets off from the riverbank, toward a gypsy camp enclosed by a circle of covered wagons, in the middle of which there are a few pitch-blackened tents. Here, a number of men wearing hats appear before my eyes who look identical to those standing beside me. And some of these men are working on copper cauldrons; others are beating gold. But already this is all wrong. "My mind is wandering down the wrong path in this game," I tell myself, "it's mixing up two different kinds of gypsy, from two different tribes, who don't really have any business together in the same setting: coppersmiths and goldsmiths."

"Hey, look!"

One of the gypsies in the tramcar puts a stop to my romantically inclined daydreaming, slapping me on the top of the head. After which he points at a sheet of paper. In spite of the delicacy of the moment, I feel like laughing out loud because fate is indulging in ironies: I went out of the house in order to get away from my pornographic magazines, and what the gypsy is showing me is precisely a page from such a magazine. A page divided into four squares, each with a woman baring her tits.

Bearing in mind the fact that I find myself in a public place, I'm buffeted by an embarrassment that originates from a blend of decency and a slight arousal of the senses, and so I quickly turn my head in the opposite direction.

The man bursts out laughing. The others also laugh along with him. Then, the one holding the page from a porno magazine gets an idea, pure genius, without any doubt. And two of them double up with laughter on hearing this idea, clutching their bellies, another two start stamping their feet on the floor of the tramcar, a fifth utters some words in their language and claps his hands, and the sixth, the one with the idea, grasps the sheet of colored paper, spits on all four corners, and then sticks it on the window next to where I'm sitting. He sticks it there with the indecent photographs facing outwards. The paper doesn't stick the first time, and so the man curses furiously, after which he collects more spittle and smears it with his finger over the whole surface of the rectangular page. Then he sticks it back up. This time, to my slight relief, the page remains stuck to the window. And the gypsies, I don't know why, look at me, as though there were no other people in this tram.

"What do you say?" one of them asks me, delighted at the image, he too giving me a friendly slap across the head, like the first.

What the hell can I say?

"Amazing," I say.

And I turn to look out of the window, inasmuch as the tram has made another stop. In other words, another possibility has arisen to glimpse a familiar face or to be witness to an event. Except that my eyes—I don't know why—remain fixed on the page from the pornographic magazine, which has begun to slide down the pane, leaving behind it a trail of saliva. I gag in revulsion and:

"Amazing," I say once more.

Fortunately, the gypsies get off, chortling, at this stop. From below they admire their handiwork and clap their hands.

As for me, as soon as the tram sets off, I find myself obliged to stand up, because I'm feeling sick. And I head to the back of the tram.

At the next stop I then get off.

⁓

"Maybe someone will steal a lady's handbag, maybe someone will throw himself under a tram, or maybe someone will get the insane idea of biting a dog," it crosses my mind. Then I realize, without pleasure, that it's stupider for me to hope for something like this than for the thing itself to happen.

I walk aimlessly, until I arrive in front of a church. No familiar faces so far. And so nothing else remains except to put into effect the idea that is tempting me, to enter the church. Ultimately, even this might turn into something interesting. Especially taking into account the fact that it's something I haven't done for a very long time. In conclusion, on a day begun on the window ledge, waiting for a suicidal urge, to enter a church seems to me ironic, inappropriate, but ultimately attractive.

I set my solemnity into a grimace constructed by means of a few exercises, I make the sign of the cross when I enter, then I kiss, plunged in melancholy, a few icons and finally, with a kind of satisfaction, I begin studying the faces of the faithful. The same sad morgue on every face around me. Disappointed, I immediately regret the idea. I don't know what I could have imagined might happen in here, in a throng of people who have no other plans for the moment except to repent with the utmost veracity. Nonetheless I think that I ought to stay for a few more minutes, at least for the sake of form.

And so I stand rigidly and yawn through the "hosannas" and "hallelujahs" of the choir, but I endure stoically. From time to time, seeing the others make the sign of the cross, I do likewise. From time to time, seeing the others kneel, I too kneel. It's not until the third collective kneeling, after we murmur in unison a Lord's Prayer slightly different to the one I remember from childhood—they say ". . . and deliver us from evil," whereas I used to say ". . . and deliver us from the Evil One"—that I tell myself God and those present really ought to appreciate me for the minutes of martyrdom I have put in. Subsequently, walking backwards, I head toward the door, making a fresh series of signs of the cross. But precisely at the moment I'm about to leave the church, a terrifying wail can be heard from among the ranks of the worshippers. And straightaway there's a crush, which stirs my curiosity.

I elbow my way through, giving up any thought of leaving, I reach the middle of the congregation of Christians, and . . . At last, an event! A wave of satisfaction breaks over me. With genuine delectation I see a woman writhing on the floor. She doesn't look more than thirty years old. Her mouth is moving dumbly, like a fish's out of water, her skirt has risen up, the tight knickers don't offer a very pleasing impression in the holy place in which they have been brought to light, the crowd is murmuring. In the end, given that the service can't be continued, the priest appears by the woman's side. After rearranging her skirt in a more decorous manner, he makes a sign to us, to the others, to move back.

I suspect he wants to ensure the fainted woman has more air, and so I move back, together with the other worshippers.

"It's plain," I hear the servant of the Church say, "that an evil infirmity has afflicted this poor woman. The Devil with his horns insinuates himself in every place," he murmurs, "even inside a holy church."

While the priest is certifying the power of the Unclean One, the woman begins to convulse more violently, but still dumbly.

"There's no Unclean One here," a voice can be heard to say somewhere at the back. "Father, this woman is having an epileptic fit. It's an illness, not the work of Satan. You would do better to help her, instead of talking to us about the power of the Unclean One!"

The priest fixes an angry look on the unbeliever who's just spoken.

"You mean to say," he answers back, "that Jesus, hallowed be His name, didn't cast out the devils from that man in the country of the Gadarenes, who dwelt among the tombs?"

What connection does Jesus have with this woman and with the man from whatever country it was? In any case, that remark was very funny and I'm barely able to stifle a guffaw.

"What devils, father?" I hear the other say, behind me. "That's just a story."

A woman appears holding a bottle of water and sprinkles the one prone on the floor. The priest tugs her arm.

"Leave her in peace!" he shouts. "What, do you possess the gift of healing? Only those upon whom the Holy Spirit has descended have the power to heal."

"But I wasn't trying to heal her. I was just . . . It's holy water, father."

But the priest isn't listening to her. He turns once more toward the one who has dared to express secular views and asks him:

"Are you familiar with the Bible?"

"Yeah."

"Let's see!"

He begins to leave, but seems to remember something, and so he says, regally, to the congregation, pointing his forefinger at the afflicted woman:

"Let no one touch her! He who touches her may summon the Devil into himself!"

The priest moves away toward the altar, the throng murmurs, no one now dares to approach the woman in whom dwells, according to the words of the servant of the Church, the Devil. Only the one who had the courage to contradict the priest allows himself to break the silence, telling his wife, girlfriend, mistress, whatever, the woman next to him, to call for an ambulance. Then, because there's nothing else for us to do, we all stand and look at the woman on the floor. After about five minutes, the man whose wife, girlfriend, mistress, whatever, whose woman has already made the telephone call, exchanges a few words with her, lets out a determined "oh well, what the hell," and goes up to the sick woman and sets about pulling her finger. She once more starts to writhe, and the man can't hold her by himself. Behind him, the worshippers are letting out all kinds of cries. The woman's skirt is hitched up again. I don't know why, especially given that no one has invited me, but I approach, rearrange her skirt and try to immobilize her. The man who's striving to pull her finger smiles approvingly at me. Until the priest reappears.

"What are you doing?" he bawls at us.

Then he pushes us away from the sick woman. When at last he's satisfied that we're far enough away from the prostrate woman, the priest shows us the Bible he's fetched, he opens it, and in a soft sing-song tone recites:

"Mark, chapter five, verse two: 'And when He was come out of the ship, immediately there met him out of the tombs a man with an unclean spirit.' And so . . . You see? An unclean spirit! Mark, chapter five, verse three . . . hmm . . . and even verse four: 'Because he had often been bound with fetters and chains, and the chains had been plucked asunder by him, and the fetters broken in pieces: neither could any man tame him.' Well, what do you say to that?" he says, addressing the man I have just been assisting. "You say you have read the Bible? Then please enlighten me, for I am unable to comprehend: how could an epileptic break chains and fetters?"

"What are fetters?" someone in the crowd asks.

The priest thinks for a few moments, and shrugs as if to say: "I've no idea! What, am I supposed to know everything? Why don't you lay your hands on a book, learn things for yourselves, you expect me to come to you with everything on a plate!" After which he starts to talk in a whisper to a young man, probably one of his helpers, sent here from the Theological Seminary. Nor does he seem very sure, but in any case he has his say.

"Aha," nods the priest.

Then, to all those interested, in a benevolent voice:

"Fetters, my dear brethren, are a kind of stone weight."

The woman on the floor opens her mouth wide, seemingly choking. The man to whom the priest wishes to prove the reality of the cursed Devil entering people can stand it no longer and, thrusting aside the servant of the Church, he stoops over the sick woman, grips her tongue with his fingers and pulls it out. Then he finds nothing better to do than to call me to his aid. He points to the woman's hand and tells me:

"Bend her fingers back."

"Why?" I say in astonishment.

"So you're talking too instead of doing something! That's what needs to be done. So that it hurts!"

While we are torturing the poor woman, the priest is shouting at the top of his voice, endeavoring to convince the multitude that there is nought from the Holy Spirit in us. "At least as regards me, he may well be right," I think. But, in spite of the fact that this might seem a grave observation, I find no reason to be overly affected by it.

The faithful around us are, however, full of the Holy Spirit, it seems, given that, at the command of their pastor, they grab us whichever way they can and hurl us onto the stone floor of the church. An indescribable fight ensues, a fight from the midst of which, after a short while, resounds—a divine miracle, naturally—the voice of the afflicted woman:

"What happened?"

Precisely at this moment, at the church door appear two paramedics, for whom the multitude makes way, suddenly putting its faith in earthly forces. The devil-ridden woman, already fully conscious, follows them to the ambulance. And behind them, I go out of the church in my turn.

∿

Some time ago, a friend, a graduate of a theological seminary, which had somehow marked him, wanted to arrange to commit suicide as follows: by sleeping with as many prostitutes as possible, in the hope of contracting a fatal disease.

"What could be more beautiful, my friend," he used to ask me, enthused by the idea and, above all, by putting it into practice, "than to kill yourself having sex?"

For a formerly promising servant of the Lord, this idea might seem odd to say the least. But only to those who didn't know him. Inasmuch as my friend viewed suicide as an artistic act, and any artistic act was, ultimately, dedicated to the Divinity. And I could do nothing but agree with him and envy him at the same time. I also envied him because he could afford to kill himself in this way. He worked for a private company (he had taken, after giving up the dream of drawing closer to God via the official route, a course in economics), he had quite a good salary, and so not a month would pass without him sleeping with at least ten women. From the station, of course, station women, who had charged less, because not all railway workers and not all travelers can afford to throw away large sums on an hour of pleasure. But it wasn't so much the low price that attracted my friend to the station as much as the fact that there the chances of contracting a disease were much greater, bearing in mind too that the women's group of clients was more diversified.

The problem is that this way of attempting to commit suicide, although alluring, doesn't get sure results.

Sick and tired of the years in which he had contracted various curable illnesses, from gonorrhea (which, after four or five doses he had learned to call "gonococcal urethritis"; he used to repeat this term obsessively, even with a certain emphasis, until, willy-nilly, I learned it too) to all kinds of minor inflammations, my friend concluded that as a method of seeking passage to the next world this was too difficult. Especially given that in the meantime he had been fired by the firm where he worked and no longer had the money to be able to afford such a luxurious death.

This doesn't mean that he renounced his decision to commit suicide. He merely found a different method: he decided that, as soon as he had saved up enough money, he would buy ten quarts of the finest whiskey and thereby die from an alcohol overdose.

"What death could be more beautiful, my friend," he kept telling me, and tells me still, "than the one I desire?"

Remembering this friend of mine, I'm now walking between the railway tracks of the marshalling yard toward the station. Why am I remembering this precisely at this moment? Because here I am, for the first time in my life, in search of prostitutes. And this is because today, in spite of its minor events, has been a shitty day. Because I'm sick and tired of days like this. Because, rather than waiting for an event, it's better to create one for yourself. Lastly, because, apart from a sum of money, I have nothing to lose. A disease can only bring me just that little bit closer to the suicidal urge I've been seeking for so long.

It's the first time I've gone off in search of prostitutes. Which doesn't, however, mean that up until now I've never had any kind of relationship with a woman of that sort. The fact that I didn't intend to is a different matter entirely.

I had, I think, just turned eighteen when, during one of my nocturnal rambles, having downed numerous bottles of beer, I met a girl. I can't remember now, and, to be honest, I couldn't even remember the day after the event, how it was that I negotiated with her to come home with me. What's for sure is that it never even entered my mind that she could be a prostitute, although I'm almost convinced that she provided me enough information to understand. Anyway, it's not here that I intended to conclude in my recollection of that event.

We entered at midnight, or after midnight, the apartment where I lived, convinced that my parents were away. So we entered unperturbed, without a care ... Amid embraces and whispers of amour, I nonetheless managed to ready the bed in my room, after which the girl remembered that, before anything else, she ought to take a shower. What followed has remained imprinted upon my memory: as I was shedding the last of my clothes, preparing myself for a one-night festivity, I heard a scream from the bathroom, immediately followed by a gruff, man's voice, awfully similar to my father's. Since, in spite of my alcohol-encumbered mind, I couldn't imagine that the girl had succeeded in imitating my father so well, especially as there were few chances of them ever having met, in great agitation I quickly went to the place where the voices were coming from.

If only it had all ended with the scene I was about to experience: the girl, shocked, wearing nothing but her panties, in front of the bathroom door; my father, inside, seated on the toilet, gesticulating and uttering words that were barely intelligible; my mother, appearing beside us from the bedroom, rubbing her eyes, woken by the ruckus; my brother, also half-asleep, repeating over and over, strangely at that moment, the name of God; I, naked, trembling in fright and shame.

But that was merely the beginning of the stupid situation in which, by the will of the cruel event, I found myself. For, in the minutes that followed, or, perhaps (who can even know?) in the hour that followed, the girl I had brought into the house stubbornly demanded to be paid. While for me it was still hard to comprehend why a girl who but a few moments before had been whispering to me words of love was now so determinedly demanding money, my father proved more perspicacious, repeatedly pronouncing the word "whore." And I, proud in my confusion and trying to defend myself, answered back vehemently, uttering dignified words. About I don't know what marriage, about my refusal to tolerate the insult of such a word addressed to my future wife, about the injustices to which they, my parents, had forever subjected me.

As the atmosphere in the house was suddenly enlivened by a general guffaw, a result of my words, and as, absolutely surprisingly, the principal laugher proved to be none other than the one whom with great pride I had named my future wife, I felt terribly offended and returned to my room in a fury. From there, I was to overhear the rest of the discussion.

Thus I heard my father say he would sooner slap her and give her a kick up the behind than give her money. Then I heard her, terribly angry, answering that she wasn't going to have wasted her time for nothing with an oaf reeking of alcohol, who in any case made her want to puke, that in all this time she could have had I don't know how many customers, that she could have earned serious money, from serious people, that . . . And, at last, I understood that, if I had caught on earlier, I would have avoided such an embarrassing situation.

In the end, imagining that the scandal might wake up the neighbors, something which would obviously cost him more dearly than a wretched prostitute, my father paid the girl. And I was left alone, face to face with my parents. But that's no longer important now.

Now I'm heading toward the station, for the first time truly desirous—and, what matters, fully aware—to spend the night with a prostitute. All that happened back then is in the past. My father, my mother, my brother are far away, transformed into memories for many years. And, I must admit, not even those memories are very pleasant. And so no one can prevent me now, at this very moment, from deciding for myself. There will certainly be no one waiting for me back home, seated on the toilet. And, above all, no one else will have to pay for the girl of my choice.

I walk along the railway tracks. A few feet ahead of me, in the semi-darkness, I notice a steam engine, probably from before the Second World War. Caught up in my thoughts, it's not until the moment when I'm about to go around this locomotive that I see, against one of its sides, something that makes me break off my journey to the station.

I approach slowly, still unable to believe it. It looks like . . . Yes. Hanging by a rope tied to a length of rail, which in its turn is somehow attached to and protruding from one side of the loco-motive, there's a man.

This is a scene that banishes all sexual thoughts, memories, desires, which makes me forget this uneventful day, which stirs in me a prolonged shudder and renders me incapable of any re-action, at least for a few moments. For, no doubt about it, before me is unfolded an image shocking enough to lend importance to a day that had up until now seemed utterly pointless: some guy dangling from a noose, his legs more than two feet above the ground!

Chapter Three

The exertions I'm making to haul the hanged man on my back are not enough to stop his feet dragging along the ground, raking the pebbles scattered between the railway tracks. I drag him behind me nonetheless, telling myself that—how much I resemble at this moment those passersby who "save" me from suicide!—here I am at last, with the chance to do a good deed. I have always wanted to do a good deed. But either I haven't had occasion or when the occasion arose I didn't feel the urge.

And here I am carrying an absolute stranger on my back. And, in spite of the difficulty I'm having in moving, I congratulate myself for the moment of inspiration that sent me off to the station, after a day begun on the window ledge and continued with a visit to church, then with memories that revolved, as ever, around sex. I congratulate myself for having had, toward the end of this day, the idea of spending a sum of money on passing the time with a prostitute. In this way, I gave myself the opportunity of finding this man whom I'm now carrying on my back. Of finding him hanging from a piece of metal—a rail from the tracks—positioned above the door of an old locomotive. And, in this way, of giving myself the right to new hope: that of saving this unfortunate.

After half an hour of strain, anxiety, swearing, but also spiritual satisfaction, I enter a medical dispensary near the station. Empty. I call out. A nurse appears.

"What is it?"

"This man here," I say, freeing myself at last of the hanged man's body.

The man I've been carrying now falls, with a dull thump—firstly onto his rump; then his upper half feels the pull of gravity and his head heavily strikes the linoleum that covers the mosaic floor. At this moment it's possible that the man may have let out a groan, but neither the nurse nor I are sure whether this really was audible. On the other hand, I'm absolutely sure that I can hear the woman ask:

"Threw himself under a train again, did he?"

Again?

"No, miss. He decided to hang himself."

"My God! To hang himself?" the nurse marvels, pointing at the patient's legs.

Maybe "patient" is overstating the matter, given that she hasn't yet given any indication that she's going to revive him.

The legs of the man I've carried here are bloodied, as can be seen under his now tattered trousers. And I don't know why the hell, finding myself in such a situation, but I feel like laughing when I see him stretched out on the linoleum. His trousers are of the bouffant kind, baggy at the thighs and extremely tight lower down, as I can see from the remnants of cloth—terylene, in fact—that still swathe his ankles. But what is truly buffoonish is the pair of orange suspenders holding up his trousers, suspenders stretched over a black long-sleeved shirt, dotted here and there with what are probably cigarette burns.

"But he can't have hanged himself by the legs!" the nurse wakes me from my contemplation.

Confused, not very well understanding what she means, I explain, almost solemnly:

"No, miss, no . . . By the neck!"

"By the neck?"

For a second, maybe five seconds, she looks at me as though I'm from another planet. Then, unexpectedly, she slaps her thigh, a profoundly masculine gesture, and bursts into a salvo of guffaws, mixed with stuttered words:

"By the neck, do you hear that, by the neck!"

Still not understanding the reason for her mirth, I laugh along. I'm laughing like an idiot, because the woman in front of me is laughing, because the hanged man is wearing orange suspenders, because I like to laugh, and because I have nothing better to do.

And we both amuse ourselves for a while, until a door can be heard to open at the end of the corridor. From behind this door appears a man in a white coat—a doctor, I think—who, puzzled, comes up to us and waits for us to stifle our final guffaws. The first who manages to do this is the woman. Grave once more, she resumes her role of nurse and, pointing at the bloke with orange suspenders, says, shrugging:

"He hanged himself."

And I, still holding back a guffaw somewhere at the level of my Adam's apple, add, in the hope of giving the doctor a laugh too:

"By the neck!"

There are moments in a man's life when he, a complete cretin, savors his stupidity in ignorance, thinking it terribly witty. And, what's more, he parades it, casting it before others as something genuinely exceptional. I think what I have just said best describes the situation in which I now find myself.

"By the neck!" I repeat.

The joy of the clown . . . The dam bursts, giving way to a new torrent of laughter. Of course, the poor woman can't resist the now almost physical urge to follow me in laughing.

And, in the corridor of the dispensary, around a patient probably somewhere between life and death (but a patient with orange suspenders), two simpletons are bawling out their amusement, while a normal man, the doctor, is regarding the whole scene in stupefaction, perhaps wondering whether it wouldn't have been better to specialize in an entirely different field of medicine, namely psychiatry.

Maybe he did specialize in it. For, in an instant, the man in the white coat manages to silence us with a single word. A question uttered in a cold, black, genuinely threatening tone:

"Alive?"

Silence, almost painful in its suddenness, falls in the corridor of the dispensary. The nurse looks at me questioningly; the doctor follows the woman's gaze and then fixes his eyes on me. I gulp, shrug, and instantly notice that the satisfaction of having saved a man's life is imperiled. After all, the man might be dead.

"I don't know . . ."

With a certain sense of liberation, after a few seconds I hear the nurse's voice:

"When the gentleman threw him down on the linoleum," she says, pointing at me, "I thought I heard a groan."

"Me too," I hasten to confirm.

"Really, that's what it sounded like!" the woman attempts to convince her boss. "He let out a groan!"

Then she draws the expert conclusion:

"Therefore, I assume he's alive."

Silence once more. The doctor is standing with his arms folded, caressing with his tongue a few strands of his moustache. The woman, stock-still, is waiting for the doctor to confirm her "diagnosis." Awkwardly, not knowing what else to do, I stoop over the poor guy with the orange suspenders, gazing at him in genuine interest. Straightaway, copying my gesture, the two dispensary employees also bend over, examining him with equal interest. And, at that moment, something unprecedented happens. As though sensing the opportune moment, the man with the orange suspenders blinks, begins to cough, and politely raises his hand to his mouth. Then he slowly rises to his feet, looks at us in consternation, reels a little, and steadies himself with his hand on the wall. He coughs again, looks at us, still in consternation, then raises his hand in a kind of greeting, turns around and takes a few steps toward the exit. We watch, frozen, as he heads toward the door. It's not until he's about to press the door handle that the doctor recovers from his astonishment and shouts:

"Get the hell back here!"

"Why?" I hear for the first time the voice of the man I have saved.

"What do you mean, *why*?"

"Exactly what I said: *why*? So that you can start laughing at me again?"

To start laughing at him? This can only mean that he had recovered his senses for a long time, noticed us and . . . Damned hanged man!

The doctor suddenly gets annoyed. He starts gesticulating, talking to himself:

"Damned lunatics! Two shouting for joy, like idiots, watching another one dying before their eyes. The third, the dead one—can you believe it, the dead one!—is listening to them, gets upset, stands up in disgust and wants to leave. So what if he's dead! He wants to leave!"

The man at the door is looking, so it seems to me, at the doctor with a certain pity.

"Mister, does it look to you like I'm dead?"

And the doctor, overwhelmed by the situation, continues to perorate, gazing at the floor and gesticulating:

"Well, yes . . . Who would have thought you just hanged yourself?"

Then, angrily, at the one with the orange suspenders:

"Why the fuck did you hang yourself, eh?"

"What business is it of yours?" he says, indignantly. "How's that, don't I have any right to hang myself, if that's what I feel like doing? I'll hang myself whenever I damn well please. I'll commit suicide whenever I damn well please, and it still won't be any business of yours!"

The doctor, with a perplexed look:

"But . . . Isn't it the same thing?"

"Isn't *what* the same thing?"

"Hanging yourself and committing suicide?"

For sure, today, which I began on the window ledge, didn't seem—what am I saying: there is no way it could have been!—as marvelous as it actually is. That's why I keep asking myself whether the whole story I'm mixed up in is real.

"It's not the same thing, doctor," I allow myself to interpose, more in order to convince myself that I'm not imagining the whole event.

"Shut up!" the man in the white coat cuts me off.

"No I won't shut up! Why should I shut up? Suicide can be accomplished by shooting yourself, poisoning yourself, throwing yourself off a bridge or a block of flats . . . err . . . cutting your wrists . . ."

"Putting your head on the railway track," the one by the door, my man with the orange suspenders, adds helpfully.

"Yes! Putting your head on the railway track. Whereas hanging is by hanging yourself!"

The doctor looks at us in disgust:

"Idiots . . ."

Then, to the nurse:

"Deal with them yourself. I've had enough. And give him some ointment for his legs," he adds, before moving away and entering the room whence he came.

Once again we are three, like at the start. The woman wags an admonishing forefinger at the man still by the door:

"I didn't tell the whole story to the doctor. He's new; he doesn't know you yet. I won't even tell you what he'd do if he found out. But you know why we're laughing, don't you?"

All of a sudden, the suicide's face sheds the harshness it's displayed up to now. He assumes a guilty look, and lowers his eyes, something which I must admit is terribly surprising to me.

"Do you two know each other?" I ask.

Neither of them answers. However, as the woman is spreading the ointment, I very well understand that the two aren't meeting for the first time. So, her merry outburst at the beginning seems all the more strange to me given that she knew the man stretched out on the floor. I wait for a few minutes, until the suicide has received all the necessary care. Then, as he is leaving without so much as the "thank-you" which, I admit, I had been expecting, I give the nurse a questioning look.

"What?" she says, not understanding, and feels her hair with her hand, thinking that is the area I have fixed my eyes on.

"Since when have you known each other?"

"Ah, that," she waves her hand. "I'm not even going to tell you, it's a long story . . . But do you know what? It's pointless."

"All the same, I saved him from death!"

This argument seems to me absolutely unassailable. If I have saved him from death, if I haven't received the least thanks for this, then at least I have the right to find out something about him. The woman looks at me indulgently, smiles, then says:

"You're not the first, in any case. I'm not even going to tell you how many imagine the same thing. But, if you really insist on me telling you, we can have a chat over a coffee. There's a kiosk here, behind the dispensary."

You're not the first, in any case? In other words, the man who has just left has attempted to kill himself before? What I'm hearing quite simply makes me dizzy. In other words, the woman means to say that this man has a suicidal vocation?

Almost trembling in impatience, I help her into her coat, and then we walk behind the dispensary.

∾

"Have you got a cigarette?"

I proffer the packet, then the lighter. She fastidiously lights up, takes a sip of coffee and, at last, asks:

"What do you want to know?"

"Everything."

"Well, no, no, no . . . I haven't got time for everything. I'm at work, as you well know. We don't get very many patients, it's true, but I can't afford to take too long a break. That doctor is new, severe. The last one was old, a decent man. I got on well with him. He died, poor thing. I can't even begin to tell you how much he suffered . . ."

"Then tell me everything you can."

She looks at me in amazement, seeming not to comprehend why I'm so interested.

"Well, it's not such a big deal," she eventually consents to talk. "He got cancer, the poor man. I can't even begin to tell you how many doctors he went to, all over the country. As a man in the same profession, he had connections everywhere, as you can imagine . . ."

The only thing I can understand is that she's telling me about the previous doctor at the dispensary, someone who seems utterly uninteresting to me, in spite of the fact that, at this moment, he is deceased. And so I stop her with calculated gentleness, asking her to go back to—in fact, no, to begin—the story of the bloke with the orange suspenders.

"Ah, yes . . . It was about him you wanted me to tell you . . . He's an odd man. I can't even begin to tell you. I've known him for three years. He lives in the depot, in an old locomotive, if you can imagine. Who makes their home in an old locomotive?"

Although the question seems to me rhetorical, I notice that she's waiting for an answer.

"No one," I say, for the sake of her going on.

"No one, it's true. Only him. He turned up from somewhere . . . God knows where. Some say he escaped from a mental hospital, that he jumped from the third floor, and because of that his legs poked up into his guts. All right, I'm not even going to tell you that, because it's stupid. There's no way his legs could have poked up into his guts. But, maybe you've noticed, there's a disproportion between his body and his legs. He has shorter legs than other people."

"I hadn't noticed."

"Well, I say it's a congenital defect. I have a certain amount of training, and so . . ."

I notice that the cup of coffee in her hand is almost finished, and I still haven't heard anything of interest to me. And so, most amiably, I ask her to let me buy her another coffee, and she, after a complaisant refusal, accepts.

"Tell me about his suicide attempts."

"Ah, I can't even begin to tell you how many there have been! But, you see, herein lies his secret. He told me it, because he's grown to trust me. Who was it who treated him after each of those attempts, go on, tell me, *who*?"

"You," I sigh.

"Yes, me! How could he not trust me? I'll tell you the secret, because you seem nice. I mean—it's no huge secret. Well, this man doesn't commit suicide, in fact. Go on, tell, me, where did you find him hanging?"

"From a length of rail, somehow sticking out of an old locomotive."

The woman starts to laugh.

"In fact, there are two pieces of rail. He attaches both of them to the outside of the locomotive, he has his own system, one on each side. Didn't you see the other piece?"

"I didn't look," I shrug.

"Well, yes, no one looks. And even if they looked, would it enter their heads what they were for? Do you know what they are for? I can't even begin to tell you, it's funny: he looks down the tracks until he sees a railway worker . . . or in any case someone approaching. When he's made sure which side of the locomotive the person is going to pass, in any case, which side of the railway track, he puts his noose on that side. When he's sure that the railway worker, in any case, the person, will see him hanging he lets himself hang from the noose. You see, he's clever . . . in a way. He sets up those two pieces of iron in such a way that he won't be able to release himself from the noose. But on the other hand, he makes sure that someone else will release him. Now, I guarantee you, he saw you coming and . . . he did it with *you*."

"You're saying that he can't save himself on his own. Then what would he have done if I'd changed direction at the last moment?"

The woman looks at me, slightly confused, then shrugs:

"Well, I'd never thought of that! I'll bet not even he has thought of it!"

I, however, would bet that he has thought of it. Moreover, even though I don't know this man with the orange suspenders, I would bet that it's precisely this risk that attracts him. If there weren't any risk, I doubt he would even put his head in the noose. I don't know why I imagine it to be like this. Maybe because that's the way I'd like it to be.

The woman slurps the last mouthful from her second cup of coffee, and then, apologizing, tells me she has to go. I thank her and bid her farewell. Then I realize I've forgotten something:

"Why 'Thrown himself under a train again'?" I shout after her.

"Pardon?"

I run up to her.

"When I brought him to the dispensary, you asked me something like, 'Thrown himself under a train again?' But just now you said that all he's doing is faking it, he doesn't really intend to kill himself. Has he tried to 'fake' throwing himself under a train?"

She smiles.

"I can't even begin to tell you, but I think the man is mad. He's put himself in front of an oncoming train twice. But do you know how?"

Again she's waiting for an answer.

"No, I don't know."

"I'll tell you how: in time and with witnesses. That is, giving the witnesses plenty of time to drag him away at the last moment. They managed it once. But the second time they didn't. Lucky it was winter, he had a thick overcoat on, and the locomotive didn't go over him, but rather it caught that overcoat with its fender, thrust him between the fender and the wheels and dragged him like that for fifty yards. I can't even begin to tell you what he looked like. I had to have him sent to the hospital. They took him away in an ambulance . . ."

I smile. This story confirms my suspicion that the man who has stirred my interest is not merely a faker in his suicide attempts.

"Well, but I'm in a hurry," I hear. "Once again, sorry. But if you still want to find out more, why not talk to him? If you buy him a drink, he'll tell you everything you want," she laughs, adding: "That's why I told you that, in the end, his story is no big secret."

"Where can I find him?"

As she's moving toward the dispensary door, she jabs her forefinger somewhere to my left, into the night, saying:

"Probably at the railway workers' bar. If he's not there, then he must be at home . . . At home . . . ha . . ." Then she laughs heartily, as though she's just told a good joke: ". . . in his locomotive, I mean."

Then she gives me a friendly wave and vanishes through the dispensary door.

Chapter Four

There was a period—it was up until about the age of twenty-five—when I used to spend the greater part of my time in various bars around town. I might even boast, if such a thing were really reason to boast, that at that time there were few such places unknown to me.

I used to get drunk in more or less all the local pubs. I made friends there with all kinds of strangers, men and women, with whom I exchanged addresses and telephone numbers, knowing that I wouldn't ever look them up and they wouldn't look me up.

I used to get drunk in the lowliest taverns, hidden away from the eyes of the uninitiated, frequented above all by regulars. Yet more occasions to strike up friendships over a glass, yet more exchanges of addresses and Bacchic kisses . . .

Nor did I neglect to get drunk in the pubs only open to certain categories of person—be it night-school pupils, be it university students, be it rock-music fans, be it devotees of folk music, be it homosexuals, be it hard-currency dealers.

There was that period, up until about the age of twenty-five, when I used to frequent most of the pubs in town . . . Strangely, however, although the bar ought to have awakened my interest, being located relatively close to the block where I lived back then and where I live still, I can't remember ever having heard of this railway workers' bar. Maybe it wasn't open back then. Or maybe I have been here before, but during one of those drunken benders that leave behind only a hiatus in the memory.

But the nurse at the dispensary showed me the way to reach the pub. And so, within a short time, I find the place where, the woman supposed, I might find the one I'm looking for.

Somewhat nervous, I enter the bar. A few railway station workers are sitting at tables, as was only to be expected. Some girls have already made their appearance next to them, again as was only to be expected. Girls of the kind for which I had originally been heading to the station this evening. And I can't help noticing that they lend a certain merry, and rather appetizing, note to this otherwise rather drab setting.

My eyes screwed up, my hand shading my brows, more as a reflex than out of necessity, given that the clouds of smoke in the room diminish the glare of the light, I look around in search of the man with the orange suspenders whom I saved from death just a short while before. He sees me first, however, and waves.

"Look, he's the one who carried me!" he introduces me to the other two persons seated, when I come over to their table. "What are you doing here?"

I point my forefinger at him.

"Is it me you're looking for?" he says, surprised.

"Yes."

"But why?"

I have no idea why. I just came to talk to him, just wanted to hear more about his suicide attempts. And even if I knew why, I certainly wouldn't tell him in the presence of the other two.

"Just like that," I tell him. "Just because."

"Maybe he's your guardian angel," butts in one of the railway workers. "Got wings, have you, angel?" he finds it natural to titter in my direction.

"Maybe on his ass," the other laborer suggests, throwing in an undeniably clever quip to break the ice.

Such quips, born of alcoholic vapors, have been familiar to me for a long time. I used to make them myself, back when I thought I was extraordinarily witty in whatever I said. This time, however, not having a single drop of alcohol in me, all I find to do is grimace in disinterested acceptance.

But it appears that the quip is much cleverer than I can comprehend, because the two railway workers set off a cavalcade of guffaws, rising from their chairs and imitating the flight of an angel with wings on his ass. I don't really understand—but nor do I make any effort to understand—why this angel would be cackling, stooped over, fluttering his palms next to his bottom. But, assuredly, they have a lively imagination, which, beyond the imbecility of the moment, has to be admired. In the end I laugh too, so that no one will think I'm a bit daft; I laugh because it seems necessary to do so. When, at last, they sit back down, I notice that the only person among those present from whom the railway workers' cackling antics did not elicit so much as a smile is the man I rescued from the noose a short time ago.

I find this seriousness of his not displeasing. What is certain is that it doesn't even cross my mind to accuse him of lacking a sense of humor. For all his seriousness, however, the merriment at our table continues for a few more minutes. I follow the example of the man with the orange suspenders and wait in silence for these comedians to find something better to do. I want to be left alone with the man whose suicide I interrupted.

Meanwhile, nothing else remains for me to do except study him: he doesn't seem to be more than twenty-one or twenty-two years old, which further heightens my curiosity as to his suicide attempts. However, there isn't much chance of my satisfying this curiosity anytime soon. He's ignoring me just as much as he's ignoring the other two.

When the waitress comes over to our table, to ask what we want, I take it as a good opportunity to gain the confidence of the man I'm interested in. But he doesn't consent to me buying him a vodka. After the woman fills our fellow drinkers' glasses, I hear him say:

"Pour me one too. I haven't got any money, but I'll pay you later."

"When have you ever got any money?" she mutters.

Then, waving her hand as if to say, "I'm sick of the whole lot of you, who darken the earth for nothing," she takes an empty glass from another table and fills it for him.

"There," she says, "but don't forget you owe me already. I don't want you to give me money, but you'll come to do the cleaning, otherwise I'm not giving you anything more to drink ever. My husband and me, we toil until our eyes pop out, but you and your ilk drink on the house, as if this was some kind of church to dole out charity to all you idle scroungers. You promised me you'd come to do the cleaning!"

The man whose age I have just estimated to be twenty-two pulls his lacerated legs—for whose condition I should, to a large extent, feel guilty—from under the table and shows them to the woman.

"See what a state I'm in? I would work . . . I know I owe you. But look, now I've had this bad luck with my legs."

"What the hell did you do to yourself? How did you flay your legs like that?"

I am expecting him to point at me, to accuse me, but he heaves a sigh, and then says gravely:

"I sort of committed suicide . . ."

Once more I realize how ridiculous these barroom discussions can be, how stupid the atmosphere is, and how it can contaminate even a sober man—I assume that the man I'm interested in is sober, given that, from when we parted until now, he hasn't had enough time to get drunk. And I congratulate myself on the decision I had the courage to make at a given moment: to give up my frequent visits to various dives.

The young man with the orange suspenders realizes what has just come out of his mouth and tries to correct himself:

"I mean, I was trying to . . . Not that I *did* commit suicide . . ."

Whatever else he might say, it's too late. How the hell could those two railway workers not laugh? In the end, if I think about it, what's stopping me from laughing? Because, in truth, to talk to someone who sort of committed suicide is quite comical. Especially if you take into account the fact that, for a dead man, he is quite garrulous, melodramatic, and, above all, thirsty.

Even so, although the situation would demand it, I don't at all feel like laughing. Moreover, I tell myself that I have yet another opportunity to find a way of communicating with the man for whom I came here, and so I roar at the two sniggering laborers and at the waitress, who is splitting her sides with laughter:

"Will you cut it out already? Can't you find anything better to laugh at? The man didn't mean to say that he had committed suicide, but that he tried to kill himself! Who is there that hasn't, at least once, got sick of this damned stinking life? He merely had the intention to commit suicide. That's all!"

My moralizing intervention must have seemed either not very serious or far too serious to those present. Because it's followed by an intensification in the gales of laughter and, amid these gales, the question of one of the railway workers:

"What did he have?"

"The intention to commit suicide!"

The fellow stares at me, seeming not to comprehend.

"The in-ten-tion!" I repeat, in a more determined tone.

Undoubtedly ridiculous to the ears of the railway worker, this word succeeds in irritating the young man with the orange suspenders. Who, red in the face, after flinging a venomous "thanks" at me, starts bawling at all three:

"What the hell is wrong with you? I wanted to hang myself, all right? Why the hell do you have to laugh at everything? I'm sick of your laughter. I'm sick of idiots laughing!"

Then he rises from the table, not before tossing the glass of vodka down his throat, and angrily heads toward the door. Then I stand up. But I don't manage to go after him. One of the railway workers, the one who a few moments ago had the bright idea of the angel with wings on his bottom, starts calling out to everyone in the bar—a number of whom were in any case already curious about what was going on at our table—pointing to the young man who has already reached the door:

"The loony has tried to kill himself again! This time he only had the intne . . . how was it he said?" he asks the other, pointing his thumb at me.

"Intention!"

"Hear that? The *intention*! Now he only had the intention to hang himself! And he hanged himself by the legs!"

Hearing the avalanche of sniggers behind him, the young man I saved from suicide stops and turns to those in the bar, aimlessly casting his eyes around the room. And I'm convinced that, at this moment, he hates all those who dare to meet his eyes. I move toward him, thinking that it would be good to get him out of this bar full of railway workers eager to find a victim for their mockery. But one of the prostitutes proves swifter than me. Reaching the young man, egged on all the while by the drinkers, she nimbly unbuttons her blouse and thrusts her breasts—rather attractive breasts, I can't help but notice—toward the face of the one for whom I'm here.

"Touch them," I hear the tobacco-coarsened mocking voice of the woman, "so that you won't want to kill yourself anymore."

Then, turning to the spectators, the prostitute proudly displays her naked chest. The railway workers' whoops of joy cause me to awake from the slight reverie that overcame me at the sight of the breasts, and I become annoyed. And when the bits of bread and cigarette ends start flying at the prostitute and, above all, at the man for whom, I've no idea why, I somehow feel responsible, my annoyance reaches a pinnacle. And so I start yelling at the idiots at the tables, without knowing exactly what I want to tell them.

Busy expressing my revulsion, in the general hullaballoo I barely notice when the young man with the orange suspenders reaches for a chair. But I do see him raise it above his shoulders and, before I can make any move, smash it with all his might over the head of the woman with the bared breasts. I also manage to see how she collapses, how the chair is raised once more above his shoulders before flying at the counter and breaking the few bottles in the glass cabinet, how a number of the men, as if by remote control, rush at the aggressor, throwing him to the floor, next to the prostitute, who is groaning as though in her death throes, her face all bloodied. And, in the outbreak of madness, forgetting to think, I rush horrified at those who are beating the young man and start lashing out with my fists like a lunatic.

A short while later, when I begin to revive from the terror that has numbed my senses, I find myself running alongside the one whose life I have saved for the second time in a single day.

∽

The fear that we might be recognized makes us focus on the faces of the passersby, even long after we have abandoned the vicinity of the station. True, there are few passersby that venture onto the streets of the city at this time of night, and so our fear reveals itself only when some belated drunk shuffles past.

I've persuaded him to come back to my place this evening; I've invited him back to the flat where I live. Perhaps I would have done so even if the decision were influenced solely by my slight soft spot for the story of the Good Samaritan. But naturally there is more to it than that. To a greater or lesser extent, it's a matter of the curiosity the nurse at the dispensary wakened in me when she told me about the one who is now walking next to me.

And so here we are, heading in silence toward the flat where I live. My friend—I don't know why, but now, after everything that has happened, even though his name is still unknown to me, even though the difference in age between us seems quite great, I consider that I am almost obliged to call him "my friend"—merely asks, from time to time:

"How much further?"

And I, somewhat annoyed by his questions, keep announcing that there are five hundred yards, three hundred yards, one hundred yards . . . And, at last:

"Look, I live in the next block."

We enter the stairwell and, preserving the same silence, ride the elevator to the fifth floor. Once we arrive in my flat, I'm overcome by the weariness of this day that began so banally, but continued so thrillingly, and slump into an armchair. And I point out the bed on which he may lie down.

He fastidiously removes his shoes, filling the air with the odor of his feet, but luckily the window is open, and so I don't worry about it too much. It's not until he stretches out on the bed and emits a number of sighs that I hear him ask:

"What do you think, did I kill her, damn it?"

I should reassure him, even though I have no way of knowing whether the woman we left behind in a pool of blood on the barroom floor is in the best of shape right now.

"You didn't kill her," I tell him, "don't worry."

"I lost my temper," I hear from over there, from the bed. "I shouldn't have lost my temper."

"You shouldn't have."

"But I was sick of it. For as long as I can remember, they've all laughed at me. Laughed like idiots . . ."

"I believe you," I nod, telling myself that it's true: any man can get sick of it, from time to time.

"What do you believe?" I hear, from the bed.

I hesitate for a few moments, before answering:

"That you got sick of it, finally."

"As if you have any idea what it means to get sick of it!" he raises his voice, annoyed. "You've got this flat, everything you want!"

"Really, believe me, I know," I counter.

This conversation, very different to the one I would have wished, succeeds in annoying me. I can't be bothered to answer the one in my bed with, "I know what it means to get sick of it." I can't be bothered, because such a reply, born of a dime-a-dozen sensibility, doesn't suit—and nor do I want it to suit—my nature. Long gone are the times when, in front of bottles of various assortments of rotgut, whose labels were inscribed, with very little justification, "vodka" or "brandy" or "liqueur," I used to exclaim heartrendingly: "I'm sick of this life!" without being capable even of thinking about suicide. Now, at least, I know that I'm trying. And if waiting for the urge might seem just as pathetic as those evenings of despair, at least I have the pride to accept being pathetic with a clear head. And he, my friend with the orange suspenders, although by his deeds he might seem a determined man, is talking the same as I used to do, quite a long time ago . . .

"You've no idea what it means to get sick of it!" he shouts from bed. "You're an oaf, just like all the oafs at the station!"

My annoyance increases at these words, and I curse myself for the stupid idea of having gone out of the house this evening, of saving this nutcase from death, of bringing him back to my place, of . . .

That stupid boredom! Those memories that overwhelmed me, memories that awakened in me a desire to have sex! My nature, forever deluded by wretched memories, my nature is guilty for all this! And then, the curiosity . . . In the end, so what if he, like me, is fascinated by the idea of suicide? Aren't other people?

About two years ago, I met a man who wanted to kill himself like this: first of all, to round up some dogs.

"There are a lot of dogs around the neighborhood. Strays," he told me. "I'd round a few up, put them in a sack, and go somewhere, into the woods, with the sack on my back."

Then he would prepare nooses for all those dogs and hang them from a tree.

"So that I'd hear their yelps, so that I'd pity them. So that I'd weep, weep for some dogs."

Afterwards, the apotheosis—he would prepare his own noose.

"So that I'd hang myself, next to those dying dogs, writhing in their nooses."

He wanted to hang himself like that, surrounded by dogs, because, he said:

"I've had a dog's life and I'd like people to say the same thing about my death: 'He had a dog's death!'"

This was a man who had quite a number of screws loose (in fact, that was the impression he gave me at the time; later I would discover that with him it was nothing more than an insipid and vulgar longing to shock). All the same, his idea of suicide, although sufficiently grotesque to repel the more faint-hearted, managed to awaken my interest. But in spite of that interest, and although I met him many times, although we came to be close friends, I never invited him to my house. But now . . . No sooner do I meet a guy tempted, like me, by the idea of suicide, than I feel the need to bring him back to my place. Damn me!

My disgust ought to stop here, however. At bottom, I'm not going to judge my new friend according to the weaknesses of which I used to be guilty, some time ago. I ought to get to know him first. I ought, nonetheless, to have more patience. Even if I don't like at all hearing him sobbing there in bed. Even if I don't like hearing him pathetically telling me:

"I didn't mean to kill her . . ."

And even if I find not the slightest satisfaction in mechanically consoling him, without having any argument to justify my assertion:

"You didn't kill anybody, don't worry."

Chapter Five

This is the position in which I start the day today: mouth open, cheeks puffed out because of the rush of wind—like in the train, when you stick your head out of the window and, grimacing into the blast of air, you turn your buccal cavity into a balloon—chin at an angle of one hundred and twenty degrees to my throat, arms splayed wide, legs bare, trembling, the soles of my feet glued to the cold ledge of a fifth-floor window.

I'm thinking that, in this world, nothing is left to the will of chance. All the stuff in existence is complementary. At different levels. A man needs a woman in order to be fulfilled. That's one level. A woman needs children. Another level. A painter, pigments. An aviator, an airplane. Bees, flowers. Fish, water. Birds, wings. A house, foundations. A helicopter, rotor blades . . . So many other levels of complementariness! How can a man be called a man without ever having had a woman? And a woman . . . How can she be called a woman without ever having raised at least one child? Would a painter without pigments still be a painter? Would an aviator who has never set foot inside an airplane still be an aviator? Without the existence of flowers would bees still go about their bees' business? Could fish swim on dry land? Would a bird without wings still be called a bird?

All the stuff that exists in this world is complementary, assuredly. At different levels. I, at a supreme level, above all the other levels, am complementary with the window ledge. So how the hell could I sever myself from it, throwing myself into empty space? How could I shatter such complementariness? How could I still be me, without the window ledge onto which I so often step? For this reason I'm waiting for the urge. It, the urge, is indifferent to complementariness, to judgments. It's pure decision, without choice, without anything . . . It's merely a moment. And no more.

Beside me, this time, on the same window ledge, now appears my new friend, the one whom a little while before I saved from suicide, the one whom I took to the dispensary, the one whom I couldn't prevent hitting the prostitute with a chair, the one who slept at my place last night, my friend who is in the habit of suspending his trousers with orange suspenders, but who is now wearing only a pair of underpants.

This is how we're standing: me, my mouth open, using my tongue to rein in my spittle; him, his hair disheveled, his eyes red (can he have wept all night?), trying to sit down. I don't even know when he appeared beside me. But it flashes through my mind that he might feel the urge. For him, there's no complementariness with the window ledge. There's no doubt about it: nothing would stop him from . . . If he threw himself from my window, it would certainly not transform this day into one of the best in my life. This thought instantly makes me lower my arms and throw them around the torso of my guest.

"What the hell are you doing?"

I'm standing like an idiot, with my arms clasped around the midriff of my none-too-familiar friend, trembling from the cold and in fright. He, not understanding what's going on, is trying to push me away. But the window ledge is too narrow for our struggle. I sense the danger of us losing our balance and, as the instinct of self-preservation dictates my reactions, I release his torso and cling to the window frame with both hands. My guest does the same, catching hold of the other part of the window frame. Then he looks at me sidelong.

"What the hell's wrong with you, you moron? You save me twice and now you want to push me off a building?"

Maybe he's right to think that I want to push him. I guess what I just did might have seemed a little reckless. His reaction convinces me, however, that he isn't feeling the urge, and so I breathe a sigh of relief and explain:

"Sorry, I imagined you wanted to . . ."

"To jump?"

He looks at me in consternation, and all I can do is answer his look with a guilty, meaningful smile:

"Aha."

For a few seconds he says nothing, merely nods. At last, he asks:

"But what are you doing out here?"

This time, it's my turn not to understand.

"Eh . . . what do you mean? It's my house!"

"No, out here, at the window."

It all becomes clear to me.

"On the ledge, you mean!"

"Yes, on the ledge!"

What am I doing on the ledge? Shall I tell him? Shall I tell him about how I come out here every morning—which is to say, almost every morning, in winter I come out more seldom, because it's too cold—to wait for the urge? Won't he think I'm too weak? It's true that I heard him crying, it's true that he spent a long time lamenting last night, therefore he too possesses a certain sensitivity, and so he might not mock me. However, in the end, didn't I find him hanging in a noose? In other words, he wasn't waiting for suicide, he was, if I can put it like this, *practicing* suicide. And so, from his superior position, my waiting for the urge has every chance of looking like stupidity to him.

And then there's something stopping me: how will I justify rescuing him from the noose if he recognizes that I too am desperately waiting for the moment of suicide?

"I came out for some fresh air!" I explain, after this cavalcade of thoughts comes to a stop.

Two comedians: Laurel and Hardy. I can't help thinking about them at this moment. I don't know what it has to do with the present situation, maybe nothing at all, but I recall a scene in which the two are about to go off on a picnic. At one point, a tray full of sandwiches appeared on my television screen. Which tray was to provide the pretext for the following series of gags. It wasn't the gags that drew my attention back then, however. But rather the length of the film: I wondered how the hell the two could be so inept that they couldn't prepare a platter of sandwiches for themselves? In other words, the fact that they couldn't bring something to its natural conclusion. The feat seemed wholly extraordinary. Yes, this must be the connection between the two comics and the present situation. Neither my new friend nor I are capable of bringing to a conclusion what we have in mind to do. This is why we're ridiculous: because the urge won't ever come. If we succeeded, it would be glorious. But like this, it is comical. Damned comical. Nevertheless . . . I still can't understand the man next to me. Nevertheless, for him success wouldn't be all that extraordinary. He was so close . . . But it was I who released him from the noose!

We both sit down on the window ledge, in silence. We are sitting like this: in silence, watching our legs dangle in the air. Like two silent schoolboys at their desk. Until the tension of the moment is suddenly replaced by excitement, at the strident cry of my doorbell.

∾

I can't help but think it's the police. The police have come looking for me before, because of my repeated egresses onto the window ledge. On each occasion—in fact, I've had such police visits only twice—I strove, with great calm, to make the man in uniform understand that I feel the need for fresh morning air. And as I don't have a balcony, the only other solution is to go out onto the ledge. Which, in any case, seen in a wider sense, is still a sort of balcony, except that it doesn't have a balustrade and occupies a much smaller surface area. This time, however, it's going to be much harder for me to explain to the police why I brought a guest out onto my balcony (in the broader sense).

Fortunately, it's not the police at the door. This spares me having to explain our egress onto the ledge. Unfortunately, however, at the door to my flat stands my neighbor, my former neighbor, in fact, the one I thought had left, to work the land sixty miles away.

This, of course, will necessitate another sort of explanation.

"Lover-boy," she falls into my arms, flushed with the emotion of reunion, "how I missed you!"

On the spot, all the woman's favorite terms of endearment from the time of our affair crowd into my mind: "lover-boy," "tomcat," "kiddy-wink," "bonny lad," "my soul's salvation," "little angel." In this instant they all strike me forcibly, especially the last one, "little angel," which brings to my mind the image of the two railway workers dancing and flapping their hands next to their bottoms. And, by ricochet, I remember the one whom I have left behind on my window ledge.

"Er . . . You haven't come at a good moment. I'm with someone," I tell her. "I can't . . ."

Her face abruptly darkens. I don't know what she must have understood, but she pushes me to one side, downright furious, and storms into the flat, stopping by the bed. She looks beneath the quilt, although she ought to have realized that there was no one under it, sees my friend's clothes at the edge of the bed, but probably imagines they are mine, because she doesn't grant them any importance, then she goes to the bathroom and starts hammering on the door.

I shake my head, a sign that there's no one in the bathroom, which causes my former neighbor to come determinedly toward me, place her hands on her hips, and thunder:

"Then where is she, the whore?"

"What whore?"

"Aha," she bawls, "so you're sticking up for her! You won't let me say 'whore'! But what else can she be if she spends the night with you? After I've worked on my hands and knees in this flat, after I've cooked your food and kept you like in Adam's bosom, this is how you treat me? No sooner do I leave than you bring another!"

"Abraham's."

"Who's Abraham?"

"You kept me like in Abraham's bosom," I try to explain.

"Adam, Abraham, same thing! So you admit that I kept you like in their bosom! And now, I go away for a little while, and this is how you treat me!"

"In the first place," I feel it necessary to reply, "it's not a question of a whore."

"Oh yes it is!"

"Well . . . not really."

"She's a whore!" She won't let it lie.

"In the second place," I eventually concede, "you didn't go away for a little while, you moved for good! And so, whether or not I'm with someone else is no longer any of your business!"

She regards me reproachfully for a few seconds. Then, without uttering another word, she goes over to the bed, sits down, buries her face in her hands and starts to moan loudly. It's not until this moment that my friend, no doubt roused by the scandal, pokes his head in through the window. He watches the scene, somewhat interested at first, and then, growing bored, he waves his hand in disgust, climbs down into the flat and goes to the bed. As my former neighbor has sat down on top of his trousers, he finds himself obliged to push her gently to one side. Probably imagining that it is me, the woman, without interrupting her wailing, smacks my friend with the back of her hand:

"Leave me alone!"

"What's wrong, lady? What the hell did I do to you? All I want is to pull my clothes out from under your ass!" my friend snaps.

My former neighbor lifts her eyes, her mouth gapes open in amazement at this apparition in underpants before her, she looks at me in utter confusion, looks once again at him, and finally murmurs:

"How about that!"

And she looks at me interrogatively.

I shrug, bursting into laughter. She wipes her tears, still frowning (reminding me that I have never yet seen her laugh), still not having fully come to her senses, then rises heavily to her feet. And, while my friend is nonchalantly pulling on his trousers, attaching his orange suspenders, my former neighbor comes up to me, takes me in her arms, in spite of my resistance, and says:

"I didn't know, my little angel, or else I'd have come back sooner. I'd been thinking that you might start seeing whores while I was away, but for the life of me I'd never have thought you'd pine so much that you'd get round to having sex with men!"

∽

Appearances are deceptive . . . This saying is too far from the essence.

You admire a beautiful woman walking down the street wearing a miniskirt, languorously moving her provocative curves, as though inviting the opposite sex to contemplate her and maybe even more. You notice some men who, led by the effervescence of their hormones, whistle after her, fling her a series of indecent proposals, working themselves up. Then you see the same woman, whom you've already labeled a whore, suddenly turn around and slap them. Yes, then there's nothing else you can say except appearances are deceptive.

You come across a beggar, who seems to have had his leg severed by a train. You believe him, especially when you see how his right trouser leg is empty from the knee down. Should you check the cripple, to see whether he's hiding his leg up behind? It's simply not done. And so you give him a sum of money, recalling the story of the Good Samaritan. And the following evening, if you're a person who frequents backstreet bars, you meet the same beggar in such a dive, as merry as can be, bacchically jigging, jigging on both legs, to a Turkish beat. And then, what else can you do except conclude, with a merry or a bitter smile in the corner of your mouth, that appearances are deceptive?

Likewise, you might hear on the news that some magnate has built an old folks' home somewhere or other. And you say to yourself: "See what a good person he is: he hasn't forgotten the needy, in spite of not lacking for anything." A few days later you see on the news the same magnate being led away in handcuffs after having defrauded a few thousand people. And then, because there's nothing wrong in admitting your mistake, the only thing left for you to do is to observe that appearances are deceptive.

All these situations have a common denominator: every time you reach some conclusion, you realize that you've been deceived. In other words, appearances are indeed deceptive, but only when you're aware of the fact. Otherwise, the same appearances can construct images (even if they're false; in the end, they say that a person is the image other people have about him; and then, if your image is constructed from appearances, and people judge you by these appearances, how can you struggle against them, tearing out your hair and screaming that appearances are deceptive?). Appearances can alter destinies, they can categorize you, they can do such a job on you that you have no chance to react. In this case, it can be said without reserve that appearances are not only deceptive but also damning.

I think I must have been fourteen years old, I was in the first year at lycée, when, after a game of football with my friends, I was the first back in the classroom. I was still wearing my sports kit and I was intending to fetch my uniform, which I had left there, so that I could go and change in the locker room. As I was rummaging in one of my trouser pockets, extracting from therein some coins which, as far as I knew, had no business being in my pocket, one of my classmates—the very one with whom I shared a desk—came into the classroom. To my great surprise, he started yelling at me, uttering, amongst other far-from-friendly terms, the word "thief."

It wasn't until after a minute of perplexity that I realized what had happened. Like me, he too had left his uniform behind in the classroom. Like me, he too had come to fetch his clothes, so that he could change. As we both sat at the same desk and as uniforms are, unfortunately, by definition terribly similar, my otherwise wholly innocent hand had entered his trouser pocket. Explanations? Justifications? My blushing at the very moment I realized the reason for his reprimands annulled them all.

From that moment, however hard I tried to make my classmates understand that appearances are deceptive, I couldn't manage to sever myself from the image of a common thief, a thief who could barely wait to be given the chance to commit a new infraction. And the following years of lycée I spent alone at my desk during lessons. Or watching from the sidelines as my classmates played football after lessons. Or reading, with the utmost passion, chapters of a novel while the boys tried to feel the girls' asses during break time.

This is more or less what happens sometimes with appearances. Even though it would be good if they were merely deceptive, the problem is that they don't just confine themselves to that. A lot of the time appearances are damning, which isn't exactly the most pleasant of things.

Right now, for example. All three of us are sitting around the table, incapable of uttering a single word—I, my friend with the orange suspenders, and the woman who has inopportunely reappeared in my life. However hard we, the men (I with great vehemence, my friend with great detachment), might try to explain to her that our relationship is innocent, all we get from her is a well-meaning smile, accompanied by:

"Oh, come off it, sweeties, you don't have to keep on excusing yourselves. My husband too, the poor man, God forgive him, used to say: 'If it weren't for you, woman, I really don't know what I'd do; I'd probably start playing for the other team.'"

In other words, as understanding as ever, my neighbor, in fact, no, my former neighbor, appears ready to accept our sexual accident (just as she accepted the other one, of which I was guilty a long time ago, the one with the pornographic magazine), without asking any further questions. No, she isn't a woman to go in for wearisome "whys," she doesn't want to know, she doesn't want to pry, she contents herself merely with understanding. And so here we all are, all three of us, around the table. She in tacit and full understanding. We in tacit and irritated powerlessness to convince.

And for me it's harder and harder to comprehend how I could have got sucked into this vortex of events, all whirling together in the course of a few hours. Whereas a day before I had nothing better to do, after my morning egress onto the ledge, than await a telephone call or a visit from the local police to redeem me from boredom, in a very short time I have found myself become a double savior from death, witness to a possible murder, friend of a serial suicide (who, on top of all that, wears orange suspenders), inopportunely visited by a former neighbor and, not least, suspected of homosexual relations. Nothing else remains for me to do except wait impatiently to see what happens next.

Chapter Six

One of my neighbors is an old man who wears glasses with lenses unbelievably thick, nearly impossible to keep on his face. From time to time, he goes out in front of the block for a smoke and tells the story—to those foolhardy enough to let him—about how his first wife cheated on him with a doctor. Then he was called up during the war. He broke his legs falling into a trench. They put him down as wounded in action. He came back home. He found his second wife in bed with a doctor. This is why he decided after the war to try to enter medical school. But he didn't get in. Because he had just been afflicted by an eye disease. And he had wanted to become a surgeon. So he gave up. This is why he has such a small pension now.

Another neighbor is a middle-aged woman. Her dog died about fifteen years ago and since then she's bred cats. First she had two cats, then three, then seven. Now she has nine. Her husband died around the same time as the dog, because he, the husband, had a heart problem. And she, although back then she was still youngish and pretty, didn't want to remarry. But not because she loved her husband so much that she decided to remain faithful to him even after death. On the contrary: because she had always regretted the moment when she had been stupid enough to agree to marriage. Now she lives alone, just her and her cats. And she is the block superintendent.

Another lives on the floor above. His wife is eighty-eight and he has just turned eighty-one. I overhear their daily arguments, of which I can invariably make out something like this:

"Do you remember, you bastard, how you cheated on me forty-three years ago with . . . ? Or was it forty-two, when you came back drunk, you pig, and beat me senseless?"

"Yes, I did beat you," immediately comes the reply, "but do you know what, night-bird? It was because you used to flirt with all the fancy officers who used to pass by our front door!"

Without doubt, they're still quite healthy if they can scream this loudly.

The former fireman, who lives in the flat above mine, is not blind. He carries a white cane just for fun. No, I'm lying. Yet it's not for fun that he carries it. But rather so that he can buy marmalade or butter without having to stand in line (the people from around here line up for marmalade or butter). What I also know about this neighbor is that a sixteen-year-old blonde helps him do the housework. The blonde is, from what I've heard, his niece. Unfortunately, however, the girl comes to our block rarely. And only for a while.

The door opposite stands ajar from six in the morning until six in the evening. Which is to say, for as long as the occupants inside are awake and can lurk behind it in order to keep a watch on everything that happens on the communal landing. Their patience is to be envied. They are an old couple who this year celebrated their golden wedding. The neighbors weren't invited.

Another old man, occupant of a flat situated somewhere on a floor above mine, constantly shits in the communal elevator. He has bought himself a water meter and can no longer afford to consume water, except for cooking. Even for cooking he sometimes takes his pan and goes begging water from the neighbors. Not forgetting to specify that it's just a matter of a loan.

"There's no running water in my apartment," he explains. "A pipe must have burst, I don't know, I'm no expert in these things. But after I call the plumber to have it fixed, I promise I'll bring you back the water."

And people give him it, because his way of asking for it— although it might seem annoying—cheers them up. And they also give it to him because they consider him, with obvious justification, an incurable madman. And incurable madmen, especially if they're old on top of it, deserve to wait for death far from hospices, not bound in straitjackets.

And then there's another neighbor, just as incurable: I sometimes see her in the park nearby, with a child of about twelve who is usually hanging around her, spitting every which way, rummaging in the garbage bins, and, when the mood takes him, making a noise like an ambulance. They tell me that the woman has been put in the mental hospital a few times, but every time they let her go after a short while. She has disheveled, unwashed hair, she is dressed virtually in rags, she doesn't speak much to passersby. I don't know which flat she lives in exactly. Somewhere downstairs. From the few words I have exchanged with this woman, I know that she's unmarried, fifty years old, and is frightened at the thought of menopause. Menopause is a kind of monster to her, behind which lurks the most dreadful threat: she will no longer be able to have children. And this is a terrible thing. She has used all her children for a time, that's really what she told me: she used them for a time, as long as they were little. She used them for begging. Then she took them to the orphanage. She has had four. Or ten. How is she supposed to know how many she's had? She had them with whoever was handy. Do you want to have a child with me?

"No, thanks."

"Come on, this one I've got here is already too big!"

"No, really! Anyway, thanks for the offer."

I live in a one-room flat, on the fifth floor. In this block. Given the things I've been telling so far, I hope it will be well understood how fitting it was for me to have a relationship with a former neighbor almost fifty years old, who used to help me with the housework for as long as she was living in the same block.

∿

I'm in a quandary: I have only one bed, in which it's not possible to fit three people at the same time. I can't kick out my friend with the orange suspenders. Barely have I rescued him from the noose, and in the meantime it's possible that he's murdered someone, and so, if I kick him out, I have no guarantee that he'll not try to hang himself once again. In principle, I would have nothing against it if he did. But not now. It would sadden me to know that I made a great effort to save him twice and all for nothing. And, to be honest, it continues to be a comforting feeling that, thanks to me, a man is still alive. In three days, in a week, in a month, he can kill himself, if he feels like it. It wouldn't bother me. On the contrary, as always in front of determined suicides, I would be filled with admiration. But, if I've been stupid enough to save him from death, then I at least want the satisfaction of him giving me three days, a week, a month of active life.

The three of us are sitting at the table. Silent. I'm leaning on one hand. My former neighbor is taking various foodstuffs out of a carrier bag: a jar of cream, a large bag of frozen meat, another bag containing tomatoes—"the good kind, from the country, not those ones with chemicals from the supermarket," as she says well-meaningly—bunches of carrots, parsley . . . And my friend with the orange suspenders, arms folded, leaning against the back of his chair, is looking at us.

After the emptied, folded carrier bag is placed on the table, I hear:

"That's everything. I would have thought you'd be pleased."

She gives me a long look. I try to avoid her eyes.

"Oh," sighs the woman, "if you don't want to talk . . . You know, I could help you. In the end, I don't think you're really homosexuals. At least I don't think *you* are, lover-boy."

My friend with the orange suspenders suddenly gets up from the table, his eyes boggling, and yells:

"Fuck you, you crazy bitch! You cretin! I'm not queer, what the fuck do you mean?" Then, to me: "She's insane, man! After we've wasted half a day explaining to her, again she starts with all this shit? She's nuts! Sort the problem out, otherwise I'm leaving."

He stops by the window and leans on the ledge.

I then stand up, my head slightly bowed. I murmur more than speak.

"Look, I want to explain something. There's no question of me being a homo, I've been trying to explain to you. The thing is that . . ."

I've always had a problem with moments like this. In adolescence, I suffered enormously when a girlfriend of mine left me for no reason. In fact, there was a reason: she was two years older than me, she had a job, and I was still in school. But after a time, she invited me to a party she was giving for her friends from work. She didn't have anyone to show herself off with, and so she called on me. An excellent moment, I told myself, for revenge. I spent the evening in question with a buxom, strapping girl, whom I chose according to the sole criterion that she was the only unaccompanied person at the party. She talked endlessly about what she liked to do in her free time. She played skittles at a club in town. Skittles! I went out with this skittles-player for another two weeks, purely out of revenge. Then, of course, thinking that was long enough, I wanted to break up with her. But every time I opened my mouth to explain to her, as cautiously as could be, that our love had faded, and that I was looking to new horizons, that sort of thing, she would interrupt me to talk about what score she had made at skittles that day, to tell me about how enthusiastic her trainer was about her future career, about how it was her dream to get a transfer to a club which would pay for her obvious talent, and so on and so forth. And so for six months I didn't find an opportune moment to express my wish to break up. And after six months, naturally, as can only happen in bad movies, she announced that she could no longer be with someone so lacking in passion as me. In half a year, we had not got past the stage of kissing. Nor could we have: whenever the skittles-player's tongue tried to find its way through my lips, the image of a buxom, strapping, sweaty girl hurling an immense wooden ball at some skittles would freeze my lips, turning them into an impassable barrier. And thus they remained, an impassable barrier, for six months, because they at no time had the courage to open and utter the saving words.

But now adolescence is gone. Long gone. Now there's need of unfrozen lips, of broken barriers. And, indeed, my lips allow the words to emerge, together with a protracted sigh:

"I don't love you anymore! Things are that simple. That's the way it is, I'm not a homo, he's just a friend, but I don't love you anymore . . . What's past is past. Now you have to understand: the thing is that I don't want to be with you anymore."

She looks at me in amazement, unable to believe it. Then her eyes fill with tears.

"Easily said. I made the decision to move back to town so that I could be with you . . . How can you not love me anymore?"

I close my eyes, trying to make my mind crystallize the image of my former neighbor in a field, her sleeves rolled up, sweating, digging. But my mind is playing tricks, so that my former neighbor appears only with a large skittles ball in her hand. A ball she hurls at my head. I don't manage to duck: the words roll, like the ball in my imagination, toward me. And strike me.

"I don't have anywhere to go back to, didn't I tell you? I sold everything. And . . . and I have lots of money in the bank. I thought that you would be pleased to see me, that we would live together here. And we could do a lot of things with the money . . . Come on, little angel!"

The strike would have been perfect; it would have stunned me. But those words "little angel," spoken in that tone that has always annoyed me, makes the ball swerve at the last moment. With the unbidden help of the guffaw coming from the innermost depths of my friend with the orange suspenders. And my growing fury answers back.

"I could never stand you calling me 'little angel,' madam!"

"But . . . that's what I always used to call you before . . . my little angel . . . and . . . darling . . . and lover . . ."

The guffaws of the spectator with the orange suspenders grow louder. And my lips open wide, to make way for words even more determined.

"Shut the hell up!"

"Why? What did I say wrong, little angel?"

I get up, waving my arms, furious. She looks at me with the tears streaming down her cheeks.

"Everything you say is bad, don't you get it? It's all stupid! Why don't you understand, damn it: I don't love you anymore! In fact, I never loved you. I stayed with you out of pity. And because I didn't have anyone else to fuck, don't you get it?"

"What . . . what do you mean? You never loved me?"

"All right, the circus is over! Get the hell out! I'm sick of being a 'little angel,' as you like to say!"

I stretch out my hand and point to the door.

My former neighbor, who has come from the country especially to move back in with me, boggles her eyes so wide that the tears that stream from them seem like overflowing ponds, lakes and dreams all at the same time. She gets up trembling.

"Get the hell out, I said!"

And my hand remains rigidly pointing at the front door.

Trembling, the woman puts on her raincoat, lets out a melodramatic "Oh!" accompanied by a fluttering of her right hand from heart to ceiling, then she heads toward the door. She pauses there, turns toward me and, amid sobs, and blurts out:

"Don't you forget what you've done to me! The ingratitude! Don't you forget that you're nothing but a snake nurtured at my bosom!"

And she goes out, slamming the door.

∿

We stand at the window. My friend with the orange suspenders and I. After the departure of my former girlfriend, we stand at the window, not having anything better to do.

I'm thinking about her. About the love that, I am absolutely convinced, she still feels for me. And I'm overcome by a certain feeling of discomfort. I had to give her up, that much is certain. I could no longer stand the avalanche of terms of endearment. Before, I tolerated them more easily. Because I didn't know what it would be like without them. In the meantime, however, following the hiatus caused by my neighbor having left town, I got used to not hearing them anymore. I got used to thinking about myself other than as a "lover-boy," a "tomcat," and other stupidities of the same sort. Nevertheless, even if it was necessary to give up my relationship with my former neighbor, I probably ought to have gone about it in a different way. I broke up with her brutally, almost violently, as though I'd struck her over the back of the head. As though she had been a prostitute and I'd struck her over the back of the head with a chair.

I'm looking at the man beside me. He's looking out of the window, frowning, thinking about his own problems. Probably about the prostitute, about what has become of her . . . But why would these be only his problems? Was I not a witness to the scene? Did I not defend him from the furious mob of railway workers? Have I not concealed him in my house? Can I not be considered an accomplice to murder if that woman is dead?

The last question combines with a shudder that wrenches my entire body. Ultimately, in the eyes of the law, I would beyond any doubt be an accomplice! Why the fuck didn't I think of that before? Why the fuck did I bring him back to my apartment?

In the following minutes, I no longer care about my neighbor, or about waiting for the urge, or about my memories, or about . . . I'm preoccupied only with seeking a straw at which to clutch, a strong enough reason to drive away the terror that little by little is overwhelming me. The terror I quite simply feel invading my entire body. Am I an accomplice to murder? But it wasn't me who lifted up the chair! No, I can't be an accomplice . . . Nevertheless, if it hadn't been for me, today the man with the orange suspenders would be under arrest. Therefore I am, ultimately, an accomplice! How the hell can I be? I threw myself into the scrum of railway workers so that I could escape! That's what I'll tell the police: "I was frightened at the sight of the woman's blood and I wanted to get out. Because there was a seething mob in the bar, I had to push my way through. Using my fists, if there was no other way." "Then, if you were so frightened by the victim's blood, what made you take the murderer back to your apartment and hide him?" "I didn't take him. He followed me. He forced me. I'm a victim here too, mister policeman!"

But what if she's not dead? Well, in that case . . . Here is the straw at which I can clutch. I can't understand why I imagine she's dead. Plenty of others have been hit over the head with chairs. I myself, when I was younger, was involved in a barroom brawl. I was on the receiving end of any number of blows. It's possible that at least one of them may have been a blow from a chair. So what? Did I die? It's probable that, while I'm here fretting and worrying, the prostitute feels fine, is earning some money with a railway worker, behind some fence. All this pointless worrying!

Nevertheless, the image of the woman collapsing in a pool of blood—maybe I'm exaggerating, maybe it wasn't quite a pool of blood—is very slow to leave my mind. And if it's so hard for me to drive away this image, I don't see how he, my friend with the orange suspenders, could succeed. Only if—I recall what the nurse at the dispensary said—only if he really is a madman. In that case, without doubt, I'll have made a double error in bringing him back to my place. So what if he is suicidal, if he's really a madman? Diminished responsibility cancels out the charm of any suicide. How can you admire a madman, knowing that he's unaware of what an extraordinary thing he's doing when he jumps off a building, when he puts his head on the railway track, or when he suspends the whole weight of his body from the noose around his neck?

The new dilemma drives from my mind even the last remnants of the image of the prostitute hit over the head with the chair. I have to find out: is he or isn't he a madman?

"Is it true that you jumped from the third floor of a madhouse?" I ask him, interrupting his contemplation of the cityscape that stretches beneath my window.

He doesn't look at me. He does, however, look down at his legs, and an almost imperceptible smile glimmers on his face.

"So you've heard that stuff about my legs poking up into my belly?"

In my turn I look at his legs, only now remembering what the nurse had told me. And I notice that there really is a certain disproportion between the lower and upper half of his body.

"They've been like that since I was born," he says. "That story with the madhouse is just nonsense. But it's true that I jumped from the third floor."

"So . . . ?"

It seems to me that there is something contradictory in what he's saying. On the one hand, he admits it; on the other hand, he denies it.

"It was an orphanage, in fact," he sighs.

He puts so much sadness into this statement that—I don't know why—he manages to annoy me. And then he continues, in the same melodramatic tone which, probably, in different circumstances would have managed to make an impression, to stir a certain compassion:

"To be completely honest, I didn't want to escape, as they say . . . I wanted to kill myself."

"Why?"

He gives another pause, and then, shaking his head, probably in an attempt to rid himself of certain none-too-pleasant memories, finally looking toward me, he says:

"Just because! For lots of reasons! But where the hell did you find out about all this?"

It's my turn not to answer, being aware of the fact that, in any case, the time for disclosures has passed. My silence doesn't bother him much, however. It even seems to suit him, thereby providing him with a good opportunity to change the subject.

He points his hand at a passer-by:

"Look, that guy has a raincoat like your girlfriend's!"

"Like whose?"

"Like that old granny you used to fuck!"

While my eyes are searching for the passer-by who wears a raincoat similar to my former neighbor's, my friend moves away from the window.

When I turn toward him, I see him seated on the bed, with his head in his hands. I draw closer.

"What do you want?" he snarls at me.

Then, calming down, he asks me, somehow pleadingly, again reminding me about the thing I would have been glad to forget:

"Tell me honestly: do you think I killed that woman?"

Before I manage to say to him a few encouraging words, words in which—why should I deny it—not even I believe, the telephone rings.

Chapter Seven

There are days—what am I saying: months!—when I desperately wait for events, praying for something the hell to happen, hoping for some phone call to wrench me out of the numbness, to inform me that, somewhere in this apparently so immobile world, something is happening worthy of my attention. But the phone call doesn't come, however much I pine away waiting for it.

But when events are determined to assail you from every side, it is no longer any surprise at all when your phone rings. Moreover, it's absolutely no surprise when you hear that the first words from the other end of the line are:

"Today is the day!"

Indeed. What could be surprising in that, when in the last few hours you've saved someone from death twice, you've witnessed the possible murder of a prostitute, you've slept in the same room as the presumed murderer and, at the same time, consistent suicide, you've had a visit from an ex-girlfriend more than fifteen years older than yourself, and, the cherry on the cake, you've dared to call that ex-girlfriend "madam"?

I myself had been thinking that today is the day: it's the day that comes after yesterday, the day on which I'll continue to have to put up with a series of questions whose answer I don't know whether I'm capable of finding, the day on which I'll be swinging between regrets and curiosity. But, recognizing the voice at the other end of the line, I realize that this day brings something extra with it: the respectable madness of my friend the former theologian, who is thinking of killing himself by drinking whiskey until he enters an alcoholic coma.

Lately, he's told me about this intention of his countless times. And I, naturally, admired him for the idea (just as I had admired him before that for the idea with the prostitutes). However, also taking into account the fact that he'd never manage to save up enough money to buy ten quarts of the finest whiskey, as he would have wished. The time when he worked for a private firm, with a more than satisfactory wage, had passed. Once, just once since he was laid off, he managed—from his dole money, which he was still receiving at the time, and from his work as an amateur dogcatcher—to put aside a sum sufficient for three quarts. He phoned me up then too. And he set about drinking, happy. All the while he talked to me about suicide. Philosophically, pathetically, but at the same time enthusiastically, as though it were a question of the supreme creative act of which man might be capable. In the end, in order to justify his claim, he went on to biblical arguments:

"Maybe you don't know," he said to me, "but the Bible presents God as having four essential qualities: firstly, by the way in which He acts toward the Pharaoh at the moment the Jews are freed from bondage in Egypt, God proves Himself to be a powerful, fear-inspiring force. Also by releasing the Jews from bondage and, above all, by the way in which He resolves that situation, He proves His wisdom. By the punishment He inflicts upon those who have persecuted His people, God manifests His justice. Then, we discover a third quality in His respect for the promise He made as regards the descendants of Abraham and in His entire comportment toward His people. The fourth principal quality is therefore love. Get it?"

I had understood the bit about the qualities. But I couldn't see what it was he was getting at. I nodded, as though I had been wholly edified.

"Proceeding from this summary characterization," he continued his idea, "we could find an answer to the question 'Why the hell did God create the world?' What do you think, could we?"

"We could."

What else could I say?

"Well, no, my friend, look, but we couldn't. How the hell could we! Let's take the first quality of God: power. Why did God need to manifest His power over mortals? Why did He have to create the Earth and mankind, when, as the Bible says, He had previously created the angels? Therefore, He already had someone He could show off His power to. Here's the problem, but pay attention: in distinction to angels, the Creator offered humans the possibility of multiplying, evolving, learning, and choosing. He gave humans a part of Himself, making them creators in their turn. And also in distinction to the angels, man too was offered the right to be disobedient. So, God's power was manifested to us as to subjects, which is what angels are, but only in payment for the war man has started against the Deity. Think about the times when God has revealed His power. To Cain, who committed murder. To the Pharaoh. To the rulers of His people, when they defied Him. It can therefore be said that His power only manifests itself in self-defense. In conclusion, to the question 'Did God create the world in order to have someone to whom he could manifest His power?' I can answer you without hesitation that He didn't. Because, in the beginning, He had no intention of revealing His power to mankind. He was obliged to do so. Well then!"

My friend the former theologian paused for a few seconds, probably to gather his booze-addled thoughts.

"But let's see," he went on finally, "how things stand with the second quality, wisdom. Do you really think that the world was born out of vanity, out of the desire of an absolute awareness, such as God, to demonstrate its wisdom to existences much inferior? His wisdom helped Him to build the world, yes, but the display of that wisdom was in no case one of the purposes for the appearance of the world. How much could the appreciation of some ignorant wretches have pleased Him, the embodiment of wisdom to the maximum degree? Not at all, don't you think?"

"That's right, how could it?" I nodded, more and more bored by his explanation.

"Another quality of God is justice, as I've already told you. As God's first creation, namely the angels, had been conceived in order to live in justice, it can be presupposed, forcing the argument it is true, that God created man in order to be able to manifest His spirit of justice. Though slightly fatuous, this claim might, nonetheless, be taken into account. However, in the very first chapter of Genesis, we discover that God declares Himself satisfied with His creation, regarding it as very good. As He was referring to His creation in Paradise, it seems quite clear that He was satisfied with what He saw at that moment. It might therefore be considered that the temptation of Adam and Eve had not been foreseen by the Divinity. In other words, not even His redemptive wish had been part of the purpose for creating the world, as long as, when He declared Himself satisfied with what He had made, sin did not yet exist. It therefore remains to be seen how things stand with the fourth quality of God."

"Love," I interrupted, out of a desire to contribute at least something to the discussion.

"Yes, love. I see you remember. Did the One Above need love, and was that why He created us? No, my friend, the angels loved Him too. So, it's clear that it wasn't a need for love that made Him invent man. Tell me, then: why the hell did God create the world?"

"How should I know?"

He was already drunk and terribly incensed, and it seemed to me that his entire philosophy had completely lost any coherence. Ultimately, after all that prattle about God and the world, he had arrived back at the same question as in the beginning.

However, although he was already seriously reeling, and his eyes had begun to dart about rather strangely in their sockets, my friend proved capable of resuming his discourse:

"You see—if you weren't paying attention? Well, didn't I mention at one point that, in the very first chapter of Genesis, God declares Himself satisfied with His work? That's the secret, my friend. Imagine a painter or any other kind of artist, who, when he finishes his work, is enthused by the idea he had and looks on the result with satisfaction, murmuring to himself: 'It's a fine piece of work.' Although he knows that the difficult task of putting the finishing touches is still to come, he rejoices at the thought that what he has before him is his own work, born of his own idea and brought to fulfillment by him alone. You see? Like the artist, God created something and put His name to His creation. And, above all, like the artist, God had no purpose, no reason for creating the world. But people have always posed the question: why were we created, after all? And, since the simplest answer, which is to say 'just because,' didn't suit anybody, philosophy came into being. And philosophy led to evolution. Now, at last, do you see why God created the world? Just because!"

After that discussion, I often thought about my friend's explanation and I discovered a host of meanings, each one of them equivalent to a revelation. But I hadn't understood anything at the time. Nonetheless, I said:

"Yes, I see. Except that I don't see what connection it has with your suicide."

"In that case, I've been wasting my breath on you. Well, how the hell could it not have a connection? My suicide is an artistic act, my friend. And, like any artistic act, it has no motivation. Or, if it has, it's not one that just anyone can discover."

And then, suddenly distracted, he added:

"That's why, you see, *you* will never succeed in killing yourself."

My indignation, aroused by the sneering smile with which he accompanied that assertion, could, I think, be heard far from his abode.

"Who the fuck made you think you're cleverer than me? How's that: you succeed in killing yourself, but you don't think I have any chance at all?"

"Exactly. Look, let me demonstrate it to you. What reasons have you got to kill yourself?"

What reasons did I have? That was a stupid question, to which I probably shouldn't have given him any answer. Nonetheless, I said:

"Do you know what I would like from life? A beautiful woman to take care of me and to have sex with me until I feel I can take no more. In fact no, a lot of beautiful women to take care of me and have sex with me until I feel I can take no more. I wouldn't say no to a hefty inheritance from some uncle in the West—not that I have one. I'd also like to be a footballer. Those footballers are the richest people in uniform. I'd probably quite like to loll around in bed all my life watching television, eating, having sex and reading. Or—aha, yes, most of all!—to invent a device, a kind of magnet, to attract all the money lost by all the people in the world. Not all the money lost throughout time, I'm not that pretentious, but, let's say, over a fixed period: over the course of a month. Well, you see, not one of these things, not one of my wishes is ever going to come true. That's why I want to kill myself!"

My whiskey-drinking friend complemented his smile with a roar of laughter.

"You've given yourself away," he said. "Now do you see why I told you that you'd never kill yourself? Because you have too many motives. That's the main, in fact the sole motive a normal person should have for killing himself: not to have any motive. Because behind each of those motives lies hidden a wish. And any wish, believe me, brings with it some hope of fulfillment. If God had had such easily discernible motives for creating the world, I tell you that the Earth couldn't exist today. Because God is too clever not to have realized the idea I've just laid out to you."

I agreed with him. And I agreed with him so much that the discussion was followed by a greatly enhanced consistency in my morning egresses onto the ledge. So, in expectation of the urge, I strove to find out whether I have wishes or not. The window ledge thus became a kind of barometer of wishes.

As for him? He drank a bottle of whiskey after that. Consequently, he got drunk enough for his sexual appetite to make him abandon the other two bottles and leave the house in search of a woman.

And, as he didn't have any money for prostitutes, that evening he stopped in front of every person of the female sex that came his way and said to them, seriously reeling:

"Would you like to make love with me? After that, if you don't like it, I can commit suicide."

Of that event I remember that the next day, when he awoke from his drunken stupor, he told me over the telephone:

"Look, my friend, didn't I tell you last night? Wishes stifle any appetite to kill yourself! It just so happened that I slept with a woman . . . Farewell suicide!"

∾

"Today is the day!" the voice at the other end of the line now solemnly resounds.

And, for all that I know what he is referring to, since the entire relationship between us is based on a single point in common, the only way I can react is to ask mechanically:

"What day?"

I hear a mutter of annoyance.

"What do you mean, *what day*? Haven't I told you about it countless times? It's the day on which I've managed to buy enough whiskey to kill an elephant. Are you interested?"

This time, although I haven't the slightest doubt about what should interest me, I don't answer mechanically, but only out of a pointless desire to banter with him:

"The whiskey?"

More muttering, more annoyance—an infantile satisfaction for me.

"It's only for me, my friend, as you know quite well. Are you interested in coming to watch me kill myself?"

This isn't a case of a wedding that you don't have enough money to go to and so you excuse yourself by claiming to have a bad cold. Nor is it a case of a birthday party, which you have reasons not to go to because you don't like music at full blast or people dancing when you don't know any kind of dance. This is a case of witnessing a suicide. And such an invitation, as everyone must agree, is hard to refuse. Even if accepting it would lead to having to listen to another interminable lecture about God and His four essential qualities and about unprecedented artistic acts. You can easily tolerate something of the sort, when you think that the opportunity of witnessing a suicide in the fullest sense doesn't crop up very often in your life. What else can we say: you would have to be completely mad not to take advantage of it! Except that for me there is a hitch:

"I'm not available."

I'm talking nonsense. If she could hear me, my former neighbor would think that she was right in imagining that between myself and the one with the orange suspenders there is much more than a mere friendship.

"I'm not alone," I hastily correct myself.

"Well, this is something I never expected you to say. You're thinking of missing such an opportunity for the sake of a woman?" marveled the voice at the other end of the line.

Not for a woman, no. In fact, not for anyone. All I want at the present time is to convince my whiskey-drinking friend to invite the man I've spent the last twenty hours with as well. Although I haven't asked my friend with the orange suspenders whether he wants to come, I'm convinced that, like myself, he wouldn't want to miss such a moment.

"I have a guest. A friend. Couldn't he come with me?"

He mutters again, expressing for the third time his annoyance in this way.

"I don't really want to. It's a personal act: you know how I see it. You yourself are welcome, bearing in mind . . ."

"But he's one of us!" I interrupt, hoping thereby to convince him.

In the next instant I can't but wonder what the hell I meant by that. What did that "one of us" mean, which I uttered so nonchalantly? Has some kind of caste of suicides been created in my mind, of which I too was an honorary member? Stranger still is that the mind of the one at the other end of the line seems to be on the same wavelength as mine. Because to my friend, who today has decided to put an end to his life, this "one of us" seems as natural as can be, given that he concludes, with relief:

"Ah, all right! In that case, I can't see any reason not to bring your guest along."

I briefly explain the situation to him, to my friend with the orange suspenders. As I had been expecting, this immediately makes him give up the profound questions he had been asking—"Did I kill that woman? Did I not kill that woman?"—and enthusiastically agree to accompany me.

A short while afterwards we leave the house. I call the elevator from a higher floor—the seventh or eighth, I wasn't paying attention—and what I see as soon as I open the door picks up my spirits, which have already been considerably lifted after the telephone conversation with my whiskey-drinking friend. The mad old man with the water meter, wearing a nightcap, is holding up his pajama bottoms in one hand, stooped slightly forward, smiling inanely, innocently. To his left, a wee pile of shit garnishes the elevator cabin.

He looks at us in slight embarrassment, then at the filth to his left, shakes his head gravely, places his hand on his heart, and says:

"I swear it's not mine!"

Of course, we laugh. How could we not laugh? Especially given that the old man, by placing his hand over his heart, inadvertently lets go of his pajama bottoms. The pajama bottoms slide nonchalantly to the floor of the elevator, revealing . . . Well, I mean! How could we not laugh?

Small and ridiculous, he swiftly pulls his trousers back up, coyly covering up his nakedness, after which he thunders, pointing at the pile with his other hand:

"See what a sorry state we've reached: burglars, hooligans in the neighborhood, louts! They come and do their business in our elevator! Such a thing is no longer tolerable, I hope that you both agree! We must make a complaint to the superintendent!"

After which, red in the face, terribly indignant, he tries to make us take his side:

"You were witnesses, gentlemen! There's no doubt about it, we must make a complaint about this beastliness to the superintendent!"

But he can't quell our guffawing like that. On the contrary. Which makes him look at us downcast, with a grimace, embarrassed, waving his free hand undecidedly.

"You don't think," he says softly, as though begging forgiveness, "that I did that, do you?"

From the way he talks, the man doesn't seem to be mad. A madman feels no embarrassment, doesn't try to excuse himself. Nevertheless, no normal person would do what he does. I manage to blurt out, amidst my guffaws:

"Leave it out . . . You'd be better off going to see a doctor, old man. There's something wrong with you: you've lost so much weight that you've become a negligible quantity for the elevator."

"What do you mean?"

The little old man is so upset by my opinion that he again forgets about his trousers.

"I mean—it's obvious you weigh less than eighty pounds. If I managed to call the elevator with you inside, it's quite serious. I'm afraid that the time has come for you to kick the bucket."

After this downright boorish remark, for which not even I can find an explanation, I make to close the elevator door. But the one inside the cabin resists. And as we descend the stairs guffawing, he, with his trousers around his ankles, shouts:

"Aren't you ashamed of yourselves, you bandits, for wishing me dead? You hooligans, it was you who made this mess in the lift! I'm going to make a complaint about you to the superintendent!"

Chapter Eight

A madman is walking down the street, pulling a rope after him. Someone, who has had the patience to watch him for a while, goes up to him and asks him, in amazement:

"Mister, why the hell are you dragging that rope around after you?"

The madman shrugs, then answers, displaying an unshakeable logic:

"I tried pushing it, but it kept bending!"

My whiskey-drinking friend also displays such logic. Although he seems very rational while planning his death, something is not quite right, something doesn't quite fit.

Even if every time I felt inferior in his presence from, let's say, the intellectual point of view, I always had the feeling that he was working as a safety valve for my complexes. In other words, there was something that made me feel superior to him, made me feel more profound. Namely, because I understood that, as far as he was concerned, suicide is an artistic gesture in itself, and not the form in which it is clothed. Which is to say, I placed the essence before the form, which is something that unquestionably indicates a glimmer of thought that has always been lacking in him. He relied—and, as is evident, continues to rely—on a logic that seems irrefutable, but one that is as tangled as can be, like the madman who pulls the rope along behind him because he can't push it. And so, if you ask him: "Mister, why the hell do you want to drink all that whiskey?" he will answer, simply: "So that I can die artistically, my friend." And there is something that eludes him in this emphatic answer: the fact that in any case his death is artistic because of its lack of any point, of any explanation for which it occurs, and not because of the method whereby he achieves it. Anyway, maybe it isn't worth beating my brains about it so much . . .

My whiskey-drinking pal invites us into his home, merrily, all dressed up, as though for a wedding. He immediately fetches two chairs, places them next to the wall a few feet away from his bed, as though for a movie showing, and invites us to sit. Then, just as jovially, he drags from beneath the bed a bucket full of brown liquor and places it in front of us.

Some time ago, it must have been five or more years ago, on the occasion of a birthday party to which I had been invited by a cousin from the country, all those present managed to get so drunk that, on waking up, none of us could remember a single thing about what had happened during the party. What is certain is that on the morning following the boozing, all the guests gazed cross-eyed for a number of minutes at the horse that was calmly neighing in the middle of my cousin's dining room. And, while the others were asking themselves how the hell that horse had got there, who had brought it from the stable into the house, I, lost in admiration, insatiably relished the awareness of the incongruity between the expensive rugs and the horse shit spread over them, between the whinnying horse and the knick-knacks in the sideboard cabinet. At the moment when they got the animal out of the front door, I was overcome by a feeling that is hard to explain. A regret which probably only constructors feel, when they think of the collapse of the Colossus of Rhodes, or writers, when they remember the destruction of the Library at Alexandria.

In a way, this is what is happening now too. The image of the expensive whiskey, gleaming in a nondescript bucket bought cheaply from some backstreet shop, arouses pleasure in me. But, at the same time, it also stirs a vague feeling of discomfort, when I think of what my friend, dressed up as though for a wedding, has in mind to do. If it were up to me, I would keep that bucket in a glass cabinet, inviting people to marvel at the sight of such an incongruity.

"Coffee?"

The owner of the bucket interrupts my chain of thought, wakening me to reality. I agree to a coffee. And while he is busy putting the water to boil, I ask him how he managed to save enough money for so much liquor.

"You won't believe it, my friend," he says, emerging from the kitchen. "For a long time I looked for all kinds of ways to save the money. I worked wherever they would have me, but I was never capable of going hungry, just to fulfill my dream. And so I spent the money. I wanted to take out a loan, but knowing that I'd never pay it back, I had misgivings. I prayed in church. It crossed my mind to go begging. But never did I think of playing the lottery. Until two weeks ago. Who would have thought it? I bought a lottery ticket and I got lucky, no joke: my numbers came up!"

"Many?"

"What do you mean, *many*?" he seems puzzled by the question.

"Numbers."

"Well, I didn't hit the jackpot, obviously. But I won enough to be able to buy myself this suit," he says, pointing at his attire and making a dainty spin that would have been worthy of a fashion show. "And, above all, enough to allow me to buy ten quarts of the finest whiskey. On top of all that, I even have some money left over. But I've put that to one side, for the funeral."

I admire his wisdom at having thought of everything, including the funeral expenses. But, at the same time, I feel myself being gnawed by envy at such good fortune. I quickly get a grip on myself, however, swearing that I too will start playing the lottery from now on.

❧

Even if the atmosphere ought to be relaxed, bearing in mind the fact that it overlaps with a number of unexpected achievements in the life of my friend the former theologian, I feel something weighing on my chest. I don't know what. Anyhow, this feeling becomes sharper the moment I see our host pouring coffee into the cup of my friend with the orange suspenders, whose presence I have quite forgotten in the last few minutes.

"Sugar?" the one who has invited us asks, as affable as ever.

"Instead of coffee," I hear my companion say, "couldn't you give us both a cup of whiskey?"

And here is the explanation for the pressing sensation in my chest! For the third time in the last few hours, the voice of the assistant at the dispensary suddenly resounds in my ears: "If you give him a drink, he'll tell you anything." How could I have forgotten? I realize—a little too late, it's true—that I have made a mistake in bringing my guest here. The other also thinks the same thing, his eyes goggling, utterly stupefied. Then, ignoring the one I have come with, he snaps at me:

"Didn't you tell him what I want to do?"

"Yes, I did."

I'm genuinely scared at what might come of the gaffe made by the one with orange suspenders. What if we get chucked out? How the hell could I have forgotten? There's no doubt about it: I'm to blame. I ought to have pointed out to my friend that he will have to restrain himself, however much that bucket of alcohol might tempt him.

"He was joking," I say, trying to mend the situation and at the same time pinching my companion's thigh with all my might.

"What the hell's got into you?" says the latter, jumping up from his chair and rubbing the spot where I nipped him.

And as I'm endeavoring to give him a conspiratorial wink, he unexpectedly clouts me across the face, a slap strong enough to knock me onto the carpet, chair and all. In the seconds in which I try to come back to my senses, reason, crammed into one corner of my mind, demands that I shouldn't react, that I should behave normally, especially given the fact that I'm not in my own house. Unfortunately, however, reason has very few other courses of action to dictate to me, and so, once I'm on my feet, I reply with all my force, punching my aggressor. In the sudden welter, I nevertheless manage to see my frightened whiskey-drinking friend grab the bucket, cradling it in his arms to protect it. This move comes too late, however. In the next moment, the one with the orange suspenders, roaring, rushes at me, shoving the former theologian, who, with the bucket in his arms, had just thrust himself between us. So it happens that, as we are rolling on the carpet, chaotically slugging each other, fighting without any well-founded reason, a drawn-out moan fills the room . . .

At that moment, as though on cue, we cease the fight that had erupted out of the blue. This affords us the opportunity to see our host on his knees, noisily lamenting in front of the spilled bucket, in front of the puddle of expensive liquor which, with each passing moment, is spreading over the carpet.

∾

We sit gloomily around the table, upon which the bucket is enthroned. In spite of the wholly tragic situation, my friend who had planned to kill himself today can no longer find the strength to reproach us with anything. He merely weeps, with his head in his hands. And we try to console him. Patting him on the back (the one with the orange suspenders). Or on the head (me).

Using a piece of gauze, we have managed to collect a small part of the liquor spilled on the carpet. Which, added to that remaining in the bucket, makes, at present, one or perhaps two quarts of whiskey standing on the table. We each have a cup of whiskey in front of us; we are each trying to dissolve our bitterness by drinking from our cups. Undoubtedly, however, someone is less upset by the situation, and that someone, in spite of his guilt-ridden sighs, is my friend with the orange suspenders. In the end, he got what he wanted. Now, without encountering any resistance on the part of our host, he can drink as much as he likes from the bucket of liquor.

Nor is the atmosphere at all improved in the moment when the most afflicted among us, my friend, who has missed another opportunity to commit suicide, bursts into hysterical laughter. In fact, he even manages to scare us when he thrusts away his chair with a shriek and climbs onto the table, and then starts to dance around the bucket. Such a reaction is anything but normal and so, seemingly out of his mind, we grab him by the legs and pull him back down.

There is no way we can stop his laughter, however. Amid his guffaws, he manages to say:

"And so there it is, brothers, ha, ha, starting tomorrow, instead of seeing to my own affairs in the other world, I'll be back to my staple trades: unemployment and bounty hunting! Because there's no chance of me winning the lottery a second time!"

"Bounty hunting" is merely the pompous term he uses to describe his work as an amateur dogcatcher or, to put it more accurately, as a man who scours the streets for days on end in search of pedigree dogs. Once he finds such a dog, my friend scans the newspapers for small ads that begin "Pedigree dog lost in the . . . area." If a small ad includes information that fits the description of the dog he has found and, above all, if it concludes with "Reward for the finder," he presents himself at the owner's door with the quadruped. If not, then the dog regains its freedom. More often than not, however, taking into account that not many dogs go missing from their owners at random, my friend helps them to go astray, without too many scruples.

"You said that you've put some money aside for your funeral. You could spend it on another ten quarts . . . So, there's still a chance of killing yourself," I encourage him.

He looks at me as though I'm from another planet, and stops laughing.

"And not be buried in the proper way? Are you mad?" he screams at me. "What do you want, for them to cremate me?"

From the way he is looking at me, I probably ought to realize that the idea is utterly idiotic. But, I don't know why, it seems to me that there isn't much difference between being buried and being cremated, given that, in any case, the act in question occurs after you die. And so I naively express this opinion.

"Look here, it's obvious that you don't know anything," he attempts to enlighten me, lowering his voice. "But I, in contrast to you, still read a few things. I've read that, if you burn, in the instant that your body reaches the temperature of a living person, you come back to life for a second. Get it?"

This time it's my turn to look at him as though he were from another planet. But he doesn't give me very long to philosophize in the margins of this idea because, raising his voice, he says:

"What use to me is another second of life? Go on, tell me, what use is it to me?"

Naturally, he doesn't have any use for that one second. So, without commenting further, I pick up my teacup of whiskey and knock it back. In complete silence, the other two follow my example.

∽

It is getting dark outside. An evening before, at around this time, I was carrying my friend with the orange suspenders on my back, heading toward the dispensary. Now, in the same room with him and with my friend who has just failed to commit suicide, I'm taking my last sip of whiskey, stretched out on a damp carpet, watching the ceiling whirl like a windmill above me. I feel sick and I'm convulsed with laughter, as I remember, with great effort, images from the previous two days. And when I think that it all began with my lust, with my guiltless (or, perhaps, all too guilty) lust to find a woman! With whom I had a mind, ha, ha, to spend the night. "See where the desire for sex can get you," a thought straggles into the others, "see where women can get you!"

"Where can women get you?" I hear, from somewhere in the room, the voice of the friend with whom I spent the morning on the ledge, or the voice of my reward-hunting friend, or both voices at once.

I realize that I have been speaking aloud, a thing which, no one can deny, is pure idiocy. To speak aloud, when your thoughts want to speak softly, I mean, to say what your thoughts are saying to you, I mean . . . I don't really know why I'm laughing, but

I'm laughing; this I know, because I can hear myself laughing, and I couldn't hear something that doesn't exist, could I?

"Where can women get you?" the voice of my friend shouts at me, from somewhere in the room, or else the voice of my pal, or else their combined voices.

"I've no idea."

And I'm being honest, I have no idea, I don't know anymore where they can get you. In bed, where else? Or maybe not. I really don't know what I wanted to say. And ultimately, what is it to them where women can get you?

"What women?"

I lean on my elbow, lifting myself up slightly in order to see from which part the question is coming, that is, from whose part the question is coming, and the ceiling tilts toward me, so I fend it off with my hand and curse it. After which I laugh. How could I have cursed the ceiling? "You see, that's my problem: I curse the ceiling. Although, I have to admit, there aren't many reasons to curse it, because it's not the ceiling that's drunk, it's me who's drunk. Avanchronistically, anachronistically—or some such word, I'm not really sure what it is my mind is trying to scrape together—drunk!"

"The women at the station. The prostitutes!"

Now I see it as clearly as can be: my reward-hunting friend is laughing along with me and moving oddly, very oddly, like a water snake in water. He's squirming his ridiculous body, as though he were boneless.

"Stop squirming like that," I beg him, "because you're making me feel sick."

As it is, I'm sick already, but his movement, his boneless-man waltzing, makes me feel the nausea welling up somewhere in the pit of my stomach and rising tempestuously toward my mouth.

"But I'm not moving," he says, "look, I'm not moving."

I shield my eyes, because he's lying; he's moving like a snake in water, as though he hadn't a single bone in his body. I shield my eyes and I look around the room for the other one. I see him weeping, like a child, weeping under the table, and moving, like an idiot, like a snake in water, as though both of them were conspiring against me, to make me feel sick. Even sicker than I feel already!

"Why are you crying, why the fuck are you crying?"

He rocks back and forth and says:

"You reminded me about prostitutes."

What's his problem with prostitutes? It's *my* problem: it was because of them that I left the house, because of my unhealthy urge for sex. But what about him? Did some prostitute give birth to him and now I've stirred up memories of being born? As if anyone can have memories of being born! I just don't get what my friend's problem is with prosti . . . ? Oh! Oh-o!

"What 'oh-o'?"

The one asking is my friend, the former theologian, the reward hunter, the freshly failed suicide. Shall I tell him? No, no I shall not tell him!

"He just killed a whore," I say, pointing at the other one.

And I put my hand to my mouth, because my words have come tumbling out and I said what I shouldn't have said.

"I didn't kill anyone!" resounds from the other side of the room.

"No, you didn't kill anyone!" I agree.

Except it's too late. He intensifies his tearful spasms and I, somehow retrieving some remnant of reason from the corners of my mind, feel that I can no longer articulate anything.

"You're the only one to blame," he says amidst his tears, "for taking my head out of that noose!"

"What noose?" inquires the other one.

"From a noose," I curtly explain, shaking my head to clear my thoughts.

Then, to my friend with the orange suspenders:

"I didn't want to take your head out of it, believe me, but when you turned up in front of me, what was I supposed to do? How could I have left you there?"

"You could have. You weren't even a railway worker, like I thought you were . . . And so you could have!"

"Bullshit! You're to blame. You shouldn't have hanged yourself! Why do you keep hanging yourself?"

He's weeping even more, he weeps and yells at me, angrily:

"But why do you keep climbing onto the ledge? And why does he," referring to my friend, "keep drinking whiskey?"

"I'm waiting for the urge. He's making an artistic gesture. We have our reasons, as you can see!"

"I have my reasons too!"

"I don't have any reasons," the whiskey drinker interposes.

"What reasons do you have?"

"I don't have any reasons," our host repeats. "Whoever has reasons is a falsif . . . a falsify . . . what the hell?"

"Not you! Why the fuck do you keep poking your nose in? I was asking him, not *you* . . . Why do you want to hang yourself?"

Silence descends for a few seconds. All that can be heard are the sighs of the one I have brought here. In the end, he bursts out:

"Because I want to, that's why!"

Then, spelling it out:

"I hang my-self be-cause I want to!"

Since I sat up, the ceiling has stopped spinning. And the room. And the other two are no longer squirming like snakes in water. But I still feel sick. Moreover, I don't know why, I feel very sorry for the one who is crying.

"You didn't kill anyone," I say, because nothing else enters my head to say.

"How do you know?"

The truth is I don't know. How could I know? I would know if I went to the station to check. If I went to the station and found out that he hadn't killed anyone, I'd know that he hadn't killed anyone. If I found out that he had killed the prostitute, I'd know that he had killed the prostitute. Maybe it would be a good idea if I went to the station to find out whether he hasn't killed anyone or whether he has killed someone—ha, ha, what a phrase: 'whether he hasn't killed anyone'—whether he has killed the prostitute or whether he hasn't killed the prostitute."

"Maybe it would be a good idea if we went to the station," I say to the one who's weeping.

"Yes."

I stand up with difficulty, holding onto the furniture, and move toward my friend with the orange suspenders. Everything has started spinning again. All the same, I reach him and stretch out my hand to him. With difficulty, I manage to pull him out from under the table. And leaning against each other, we head toward the door.

"Leaving?" the voice of our host can be heard from behind.

"Yes," I nod. "Leaving."

Chapter Nine

As I walk, my steps are mechanical, under the influence of the alcohol and of a feeling probably similar to that felt by a fighter before a battle. I'm not even thinking about the reason for which I'm heading toward the station. My steps are led only by the desire to find out, once and for all, what the hell happened the evening before, that cursed evening when I met my friend with the orange suspenders. The faces of the passersby are blurred by night, by alcohol, by insensibility. Not one of them imprints itself on my mind.

When I was five or six or seven years old, I used to play with matchsticks in the house. All children do it, but I like to think that I used to do so differently than the other children. I'd draw a line with a pen in the middle of the matchsticks, until I had about twenty with lines drawn through the middle. Then I'd take two matchsticks, whose heads were in the best condition, and color them in: one from the middle down, the other from the middle up. These were the generals. They would lead the fearsome army of matchsticks with a middle stripe to glorious victories over the enemy. The enemy . . . The enemy was represented by other matchstick soldiers, which, as a sign of their evil, had burnt heads. The battles would last from morning to night, and unfold on water, in the mountains, and in the jungle. The blue Persian rug in the middle of the room, on which the warships floated—these were in fact two books: *The Adventures of Muddle-Head*, a hardback with glossy blue cardboard, which represented the vessel of the good guys, and *Pinocchio*, a paperback, the bad guys' ship, which couldn't sail as fast—was the sea. The quilt, with its rolling bulges, would become a mountainous region, with unsuspected gullies and chasms, in which my matchstick characters would break their necks. And the silver fox fur, which mother had placed—I never understood for what reason—at the foot of the bed, became a vast jungle. Not a very green one, it's true, but my imagination passed over this obstacle. What is important is that I fused so completely with the characters that I'd feel the tempests I invented for them, I'd feel seasick floating on the blue *Muddle-Head*, I'd shiver with cold when the quilt was cloaked in harsh snows, and I'd take fright when some blood-thirsty lion made its appearance from behind a dusky tuft of silver fox fur.

I don't know how the connection came about (probably because of the alcohol I've drunk), but the sensations I feel now, as

I head to the station alongside my friend, are similar to those I used to feel back then, in childhood. The faceless passersby bear a striking resemblance to my burnt-headed matchsticks, the street along which I numbly walk sends my thoughts off to the numbness that would overwhelm me when I used to "march" over the peaks of my quilt, and the determination with which we're now heading to the station seems reminiscent of the two generals of the matchstick army.

After about half an hour's walk, maybe more, I start to come round from my drunkenness. My friend with the orange suspenders also comes round, to a certain extent: the fresh air is gradually restoring the frown I've grown used to during our short time together, replacing the mute drunken lack of expression of the last hour.

We head to the station, in silence . . . I haven't yet thought about how we're going to find out what was the result of everything that happened in the railway workers' bar last night. It's only now, as the station begins to loom from the darkness, that I raise this problem. Quite simply to go into the bar and ask would, obviously, be stupid.

I'm glad that the way from my whiskey-drinking friend's house has been so long, giving us an opportunity to clear our heads. If the distance had been shorter, we probably wouldn't have thought about not entering that bar. And, more than likely, there we would have been beaten up by the railway workers. Or, if the worst-case scenario is true, the one in which the prostitute is dead, we would have been arrested in a very short time—he as perpetrator of the crime, I as his accomplice. Even though I played no part in lifting that chair and breaking it over the head of that poor woman, I'm no longer drunk enough to imagine that the police would let me off. Beyond any doubt, I became an accomplice at the moment I rescued him from the hands of the railway workers and hid him in my house.

Reaching the last block before the station, I signal my friend to wait. He stops, astonished.

"Everybody at the station knows you, don't they?"

He agrees, but he doesn't seem to understand the reason why I don't want him to come with me.

"Then why the fuck would you go there?" I explain. "Do you want them to kill you?"

He shrugs, indifferently. Nonetheless, he remains where he is at the moment I move away.

∾

My head lowered, because I'm afraid of being recognized, I head toward the railway workers' bar. I avoid each person heading in my direction, looking the other way, shivering, although it's not less than sixty degrees outside. It's not because of the cold that I'm shivering.

Reaching the building whose memory stirs no pleasure in me, I try to peer in through the large windows. In spite of the grimy panes, I can tell that, apart from the waitress and the barman—her husband, as far as I recall—there's no one else in the pub, which worries me. But it doesn't worry me for long because I find the explanation I come up with to be satisfactory. Namely, following the brawl last night, the pair have probably decided to clean up, closing the bar for a day.

Given that here doesn't seem to be the place where I can find out anything about the fate of the woman walloped by my friend, I head toward the passengers' station, hoping to come across some prostitute who might be able to give me some answers.

My hopes are not dashed. Right by the station building, a number of girls, leaning against the wall, are smoking cigarettes, waiting for customers. I see one standing a little way from the group, and, concealing myself in a darker spot, I call her over, in a whisper. She looks all around her, but not at me, and so I have to emerge from the shadows somewhat, so that she will see me. In the end, she looks in the right direction, but at the same time a few of the other girls look my way too. The one I called comes over, smiling. Giving me a look that would indicate she understands why I'm hiding in the dark, she says:

"Not embarrassed are you, handsome? Don't be. Relax. The girls over there," she points at the others, "are all in the same line of work as me."

"That's not what I'm here for," I continue to speak in a whisper. "I'd like you to clear up a certain matter for me."

The girl suddenly frowns, pouts in disgust and makes to turn her back on me. At that moment I see the others whispering together and then coming toward us. And so there's nothing else for it, I lay one hand on the prostitute and say:

"Come on, I'll pay."

Then I drag her after me.

"You're in a real hurry!" she observes, trying to keep up with me. "First you say you don't want to, then you start acting like it's bursting out of your trousers."

I don't answer her, as I am too preoccupied with getting far enough away from the other girls, amongst whom some were very possibly in the bar last night. After no more than fifteen paces, however, the girl stops, pointing to a public lavatory.

"Here it is," I hear.

"Here *what* is?"

"Where do you want to take me, back to your place? Not likely!" she raises her voice. "How do I know you're not some murderer, or who the hell knows what, some pervert who'll call another ten guys to have their way with me? Back at your place you can do whatever you like with me, and I won't be able to defend myself. So I'm not going!"

I understand that this public toilet is the place in which the sex act is to take place. And I also understand that the woman next to me is about to make a scene. Bearing in mind all these, I think the wisest decision would be not to be picky. And to agree to her terms.

In spite of the fact that my head hasn't completely cleared after this evening's drinking bout, I nonetheless manage to understand that the lavatory attendant's knowing smile the moment I thrust, at the behest of my companion, some money into his hand, is rather humiliating for me. However, I feel even more humiliated when, once inside a cubicle, the girl stretches out her hand, demanding a certain sum of money.

"I'm not doing anything until I'm sure you're honest," she says. "When I was younger and dumber, I used to take the money afterwards, because I was too trusting. Except some of them ran off, after they'd had their way, and I'd be left with nothing."

I remember yesterday evening, when I went out with the thought of doing exactly what she's now offering. I feel like bursting into laughter, realizing how stupid, how lacking in pleasure the whole scene is. I feel like laughing even more when I think that I would definitely prefer to be in my own room right now, in front of some pornographic magazine, than here, in a toilet cubicle, with a grim-faced girl in front of me, waiting with outstretched palm to give her money.

Without pleasure, I count the money into her hand. And I notice how, each time I place some in her palm, the smile spreads wider across her face.

"For this money," she says, in satisfaction, "I'm going to give you the full service."

It was almost all the money I had. There's barely enough left in my pocket to cover the cost of my food for the next two or three days. However, because there'd be no point in complaining, given that I can't summon up sufficient sensitivity for such a thing in here, I ask what the girl means, in the present situation, by the "full" service.

"That's normal and oral," she explains plainly and, as it seems to me, with a certain candor.

By the way she's talking, she manages to make any reservations I might have had when I came in here slowly vanish. And so I'm glad for the opportunity which, by her words, she gives me to crack a joke.

"It's only the oral service I'm after."

She's surprised, then frowns:

"All right, if that's all you want . . . But I'm telling you, let's be clear: now that you've given me the money, I'm not interested in what you want. You've handed over the money, it's mine now."

"I just want to talk," I explain, attempting a well-meaning smile. "It was a joke: oral, meaning *talking*."

"Oral means with the mouth, idiot."

"Well, yes. Don't you talk using your mouth?"

For her it seems nothing more than a lame joke. And, if I think about it, it is for me too. All the same, I don't know how, but, even though I have every reason to be completely annoyed about the situation—I'm in a public toilet waiting for a prostitute to tell me whether another prostitute died following an attack to which I was an unwilling accomplice—I find myself, all of a sudden, well disposed.

"What are you, one of those impotent freaks who just wants to hear me talk dirty?"

I continue to smile like an idiot, without answering her.

"All right," she sighs, "I can do that stuff too. But if that's what you want, the price is still the same. It's as much of a perversion as anything else."

Somehow disappointed, she leans against the cubicle wall, asks me for a cigarette, lights it, then, blowing the first puff in my face, asks:

"What do you want me to say? How I did it the last time, with an Arab, or how I did it the first time, with a boyfriend of mine?"

I realize that the girl has a story ready even for such cases as this, which, once more, instead of irritating me, enhances my good disposition. Nevertheless, even though the part with the story of her past affairs seems interesting, I ought, perhaps, to rein in my curiosity. Especially in view of the fact that otherwise I'll miss out on the discussion I've come here for.

Speaking of the discussion I've come here for . . . This thought brusquely makes me wake up from the pleasant state in which

I've almost recklessly allowed myself to sink. And, as soon as this happens, the girl whom my imagination had endowed with a certain candor and whom I had even begun to view with sympathy reverts to her image of a mundane prostitute, who interests me only through the prism of the information she might be able to offer me. I curse my momentary slackness and stop her from going into details about her sex life.

"What the hell do you want, then?" she barks, reaching the limit of her patience. "Aren't you interested in how I did it with an Arab! How I did it with my first boyfriend! Not even that! Or do you want me to tell you how I do it with women? Or . . ."

She stubs her cigarette out against the wall with a jabbing movement, the cigarette on which she's only taken a couple of drags. After which she makes visible efforts to calm down, and asks me:

"Or have you changed your mind? Do you want what all normal people want?"

Without waiting for an answer, without even looking at me, she shoves her hand up my sweater, touching my skin. Her gesture, even though it ought to create a different sensation, irritates me. I angrily push her away, with enough force to make her look at me in fright:

"There are people to protect me, you know!" she says, raising her voice. "I've got someone to protect me! I only have to scream, he'll be here as fast as a bullet and break your legs."

I try to calm down and, at the same time, calm her down.

"There's something I want us to talk about," I tell her, in an almost gentle tone. "I want to know . . . to find out . . ." I stutter, not knowing how to broach the subject, "to find out about a colleague of yours."

"I'm not saying nothing about my colleagues!" the girl rebuffs me determinedly, even though she has no idea what I'm talking about.

Then, her face clouding:

"Hey, are you a cop?"

"How could I be a cop?" I shake my head vigorously. "What the fuck—do I look like a cop?"

"Then why are you shouting at me?"

Her consternation is growing. And I feel like I'm suffocating inside this toilet cubicle, as I realize I might have squandered the money I've given to the girl, I might have missed out on the opportunity to have sex with her, and I might be left without any information. This possibility becomes all the more sharply defined the moment in which, taking advantage of my confusion, she opens the door and steps outside the cubicle.

Completely desperate, seeing her walk away, the only thing that passes through my mind is to take down my trousers and stretch out my hands toward the prostitute, as though I had just decided to open the gates of Paradise, and call her back.

An absolutely ridiculous scene were there to be a witness, which, fortunately, there is not: I, embracing her from afar, with my trousers around my ankles; she, scowling, her eyes fastening on my bared groin, then bursting into laughter; I, puzzled, lowering my hand, pointing my forefinger at what is on offer; she, now splitting her sides, raising her right hand and likewise pointing her finger at what is on offer; I, looking down and, instantly embarrassed by the paucity of inches; she, waving the middle finger of the same right hand at me, departing extremely well-disposed.

After pulling up my trousers and hurriedly buttoning up, I run after the girl.

I feel humiliated by everything that has taken place. Downcast because I haven't been able to find out anything. And saddened by the stupidity I've shown. However, as if all that weren't enough, at the toilet door the girls I saw a few minutes ago leaning against the station wall are waiting for me. And, whereas they take no notice of the girl who emerges before me, as soon as they see me a few of them begin to shout:

"That's him, yes, that's him!"

That's who? What the hell do they mean?

"You were in the bar last night!"

They don't give me any time to come to my senses. As though on cue, they start screaming like a horde of banshees—a drawn-out keening, of which I seem to make out: "poofterwankersyphiliticmoronnutcase . . ." ". . . ucking impotent . . ." "Madman!" "Bastard!"—and they start flailing punches at me. I don't know how, but I manage to escape from their clutches. Then I run back toward the block where I left my friend with the orange suspenders, to the sound of furious screams. Which slowly fade away, however.

∾

There is no longer anybody in front of the block. I swear and am about to continue running. But I don't get very far. Because he looms up in front of me unexpectedly, frightening me. Emerging from behind some bushes. His face contorted with emotion. His eyes bulging. His hand pressed to his heart.

"What happened?" he asks, barely managing to articulate the words.

"Damn you!"

"Why? Did I kill her?"

The girls weren't able to keep up with me, I left them somewhere way behind, and, as far as I can see, they've even given up trying to chase me. And so I calm down, resting my hands on my knees, trying to catch my breath.

"Damn you for scaring me," I explain my curse. "What got into you, hiding behind the bushes?"

"I was hiding."

"*Why*?"

"So that they wouldn't find me!"

"Who?"

"What do you mean *who*? Them, the railway . . . Leave me alone, damn it, will you! Do you think I care about your questions right now? Better tell me what happened! Why the hell did it take you so long to get back? I killed her, didn't I?" he is almost screaming.

His eagerness to find out, although justified, is annoying me. Especially given that I don't have any answer to his question. How am I supposed to know whether he killed her or not? I ought to have found out, but . . . In the end, it wasn't me who hit the prostitute over the head! And so, rightly speaking, I don't owe him any answer. He ought to have controlled his temper that night, and today I wouldn't have had to flee like an idiot, chased by a horde of madwomen. How am I supposed to know if he killed her? Was there anyone I could have asked?

However, because I have no wish for him to think I'm incompetent, in spite of the fact that—it would have been obvious to anyone at all—I was by no means lacking in competence back there at the station, I say:

"It was hard to find anyone who knew anything, that's why it took so long. But in the end I found out."

I see his face transfigured, the emotion, reaching paroxysm, furrowing his face with lines of complete despair, and so, forcing a smile, I say:

"No need to worry, you didn't kill anybody."

Chapter Ten

It's well understood that this is the position in which I start the day today: mouth open, cheeks puffed out because of the rush of wind—like in the train, when you stick your head out of the window and, grimacing into the blast of air, you turn your buccal cavity into a balloon—chin at an angle of one hundred and twenty degrees to my throat, arms splayed wide, legs bare, trembling, the soles of my feet glued to the cold ledge of a fifth-floor window.

A ritual. Everything has already become a comical ritual, in expectation of the suicidal urge. Unfortunately, as ever, it doesn't want to come. And so, what else remains for me to do except gaze, almost devoid of feeling, of emotion, at the cement buildings that stretch out beneath (or parallel to) me? Buildings hewn in the form of cubes. Cubes pierced by monotonous squares. Squares through each of which can be glimpsed, even at this early-morning hour, a man. A man preparing food. A man struggling to hang curtains. A man taking a bite of something. A man putting his hand up his wife's skirt. A man scratching his crotch. People who are like paintings, with the simplest of titles. People who live like idiots, because they can't do otherwise.

Nevertheless, ultimately there is a feeling. Of wonderment. Wonderment that originates in a sort of revelation: look, there's a man, a window, a block; look lower, there's that road with a yellow streak down the middle; look, there are some cars going up and down, small, medium, large cars, transporting people, who transport cement, who transport metalwork; look, damn it, there's even an airplane flying overhead! And all these proceed from a wretched scene, from the depths of time. A scene which, I don't know how, begins to unfurl before my eyes: two animals, face to face; one sinewy, with snarling fangs, resting on all fours; the other, lifted up by destiny to stand on two legs, suffering from a backache, intuiting that it's going to lose this fight; and then, as though in a film, in which the sequences are in slow motion to heighten the drama, the latter animal, the one on two legs, bends down, picks up a rock, and hurls it at the former's head; then it takes another stone and another . . . From bending down, from picking up a rock, man emerged. If I'm to go by scientific, atheistic theories.

Then came evolution. Mankind first evolved by counting rocks, as many rocks as possible. Then bear skins. Then, responding to aesthetic criteria, more beautiful leopard skins.

Gradually, mankind went from skins to woven fabrics. And, continuing to evolve, at a given moment fancy dress balls appeared. Firstly at the court of the pharaohs, then at the courts of the aristocrats. Many other important objects appeared: barrels for wine, head-scratchers (whereby the effects of lice bites were banished) holders for various perfumes and bath salts, pails whereby water was carried to the bathrooms of blue-blooded young ladies, hats, fishing rods, fly and mosquito swatters, twenty types of fork, hat bows, and many more. At a given moment, the meat grinder appeared.

How wonderful this invention must have seemed: the meat grinder! I can even imagine the first people to have benefitted from it. I can imagine the men with their faces puffy from alcohol, I don't know why I see them like this, looking stupidly at their wives, as the latter thrust greenish-red chunks of beef into the upper part of the grinder. Then I see the wives, turning the handle of the grinder with muffled grunts, as the sweat trickled down their breasts that seem to burst under the pressure of their linen blouses, their hair disheveled, the grease stains on their faces completing the image of the perfect housewife, and their large bottoms moving rhythmically on the stool next to the meat grinder. The man, woman and, above all else, the minced meat emerging symmetrically through the perforations of the grinder, like red caterpillars . . .

Closer to our own times, the cooker and refrigerator (especially the latter) have become the kings of technology, surpassing the stage of the dreams that mankind had to cram for thousands of years into one corner of the fantastical. The fantastical became reality at the most important moment in the development of human society: at the moment when the world's population, having reached, in just a few years, the situation in which it numbered between one and two billion people, and in another few years between two and five billion, lived beneath the specter of universal hunger. And, precisely when the struggle for food seemed to be underway, the situation was solved by the invention of these two objects, efficient weapons in reducing waste. But most important of all is the fact that, together with these two objects, new-style ladies also appeared, the ones who, fastidiously fluttering their handkerchiefs, which afflicted men's noses with highly evolved perfumes, gesticulated in societal endearment, saying:

"I can't bear to see animals being slaughtered. I eat meat, it's true, but all I do is buy it and keep it in *mon réfrigérateur*."

Or:

"My favorite food? Oh, I adore making the renowned *coq au vin* in the oven of my new cooker, with a delicious side-helping of nice and brown *pommes de terre*."

I'm laughing like an idiot on the window ledge, thinking about all these. I laugh, then I turn my eyes once more to observe the view, admiring the cityscape that presents itself to me. The cityscape of the present.

A present that's subject to electricity, the last and perhaps single greatest invention of mankind, a present with calculators and electric peppercorn grinders, with pregnancy tests that turn red to announce children or abortions, with training shoes packed with little orange, green and blue twinkling bulbs, like a Christmas tree whose fairy lights play *Für Elise*, with cooking pots that make the food unaided, with televisions and photocopiers . . . This baneful present, with its cement buildings. Buildings hewn in the shape of cubes. Dully punctured by square windows. Windows through each of which can be seen, even at this early-morning hour, a man. A man finishing the preparation of food. A man losing his temper and tossing a curtain away. A man drinking a glass of water. A man undressing his wife. A man no longer scratching his crotch. People like paintings, with the simplest of titles. Ultimately, people living like idiots, because they can't do otherwise.

And me. Standing on my ledge and thinking of people, as though I weren't a person myself.

∿

Interrupting my excursus into the history of mankind, my friend with the orange suspenders sits down next to me. For a few moments, in silence, he swings his legs back and forth, pensively, somewhat gloomily. But, I imagine, in a state of mind with less philosophical pretensions than the one in which I myself am sunk.

"If I killed her," he finally starts to say, "I would have jumped off this ledge right now, without hesitation. I wouldn't have joked around; I wouldn't have wanted anyone to save me. I would have jumped, period."

Then, abandoning his gloomy mien, looking at me, the one who's barely just returned to the everyday world:

"What're we going to do today?"

It's not that long since sunrise, and so I don't yet know what we're going to do today. If it were only up to me, I wouldn't do anything except lie in bed and stare at the walls. Except day-dream and think about people as though I weren't a person myself. That's all. I feel like staring at my walls, lying in bed, as long as I am still able.

"If we've got nothing else to do," I hear, "what do you say we go to my locomotive?"

"Why?"

My friend smiles mysteriously, pointing to his throat with his forefinger. At last, seeing that I don't understand what he's trying to convey by this sign, he explains:

"Can't you think with that head of yours? We could hang ourselves as soon as we spot someone approaching."

"Kill ourselves?"

"No, man. We'll just pretend."

At last, I get the idea. And, given that he found it appropriate to make this proposal by means of signs, I answer in the same manner. Except that I point my forefinger at my temple.

"That way," he ignores me, "the railway workers would think that we're sorry about that stuff at the bar, get it? That we regret beating up the prostitute and that that's why we want to kill ourselves. And maybe like that they'll forgive us."

"We regret beating her up? We?" I exclaim. "You beat her up, I didn't even go near her!"

My objection amuses him. And nor does he have any reason to react otherwise. Without a care, he even allows himself to make me a concession, a large piece of large-heartedness.

"All right, only I beat her up. What does it matter? As long as she's not dead, who cares which of us hit her over the head? If she's dead, then there's lots who'll be interested. But even then, you at least have to admit that we're both involved: me—the killer, you—because you were with me and you hid me . . . What do they call it? An accomplice, ain't it?"

He gives me a wink and then jumps off the ledge back into the room. The situation is stupid. Keeping to myself my uncertainty as regards the consequences of the blow the prostitute took to the head from the chair, I conjure up images of prison-cell bars, of buggery in the showers, of all kinds of tattooed killers, and of murders tolerated by the warders.

These macabre images make me tremble all over. But precisely this tremor, clear proof of the weakness of which I'm guilty, awakens in me objection. An objection that almost leads me to confess that in fact I have no idea whether she's dead or not, that I found out nothing last night. Ultimately, the right thing to do would be to tell him. Why should only I think about the history of the world, when I don't feel like it all? Why should only I include people in paintings with the simplest of titles? Why should only I do all these things, to rid my mind of black thoughts, while he doesn't have a care, convinced as he is that the prostitute is still alive?

However, I'm left on the verge of telling him the truth . . . Because, just as they're about to come out, my words get tangled up somewhere in my throat. Not because of some hesitancy born of compassion. In the fury that's overwhelmed me, I couldn't care less how he would react. Something else stops me. Namely the image I have glimpsed out of the corner of my eye, even before I turn around toward my friend. An image which only now strikes me, with a delayed reaction. Slowly, hoping that it was a phantasm caused by my fears, I leave the one in the room to the will of fate and lean out of the window, gazing toward the ground floor of the block.

To my great disappointment, I didn't have the fortune to be mistaken: through the front door to the building in which I live two policemen are about to enter.

∾

I have often posed myself the following question: what do the passengers of an airplane that's about to crash feel in the minutes—or seconds—of life they still have left? How is it for them: a frantic search for a place to hide, maddened screams, total confusion? Or silence? Or resignation in the face of the inevitable?

The answer seems to have provided itself to me now, when it interests me very little. The entry of the two policemen into my block causes me to search frantically for a place in which to hide. No longer thinking of anything, I look around me in confusion, then scream at the other one not to open the door, "Who to? Who to?" he loses his patience, "Not to anybody!" I run to the kitchen, as though in there I'll find salvation, I come back, stop in the middle of the room, insanely look around me and, in the end, collapse on the bed, resigned. Then I'm touched by a glimmer of hope that they've come here, to my block, looking for someone else. For some other reason.

"Have you gone mad? Who shouldn't I let in?" the man principally responsible for my present state asks once more.

Even if I wanted to reply, I'd no longer have time. Knocking can be heard at the door, then the doorbell. No, they haven't come looking for someone else, for some other reason . . . I stand up, trembling, and, suddenly having become religious, make the sign of the cross. Then I open the door.

One of the policemen is speaking to me, with a stern face. I know he's talking to me because I can see his lips moving. But I can't understand virtually anything of what he's saying. I understand only that he's pronouncing my name, then another name, which sounds terribly familiar, but I'm in no condition to recognize it, in no condition to arrange the words I'm hearing in any logical order. Moreover, the only words I'm able to articulate at this moment are:

"Thank you."

When the one who's been speaking to me grimaces, somehow thrown off balance, I realize that I haven't used the most suitable greeting.

"Good day," I correct myself.

The policeman puts his hand in his pocket, which, in my desperation, makes me imagine that he's about to pull out a pistol. But he holds out a photograph from which a woman is smiling at me. A few seconds pass before I discover in this photograph my former neighbor, the one whom I told I didn't love.

"Do you recognize her from this photograph?"

"Aha," I manage to mumble.

The policeman, with a grave face, says something else to me, but not even now am I listening. I'm not listening to him because only now do I realize that there are small chances of my former neighbor and the woman hit over the head with the chair being in any way connected, and the joy that overwhelms me is almost as violent as my terror was shortly before.

"We didn't find on her any papers by which to identify her," I hear at last. "In her purse she didn't have anything except some money and your identity card."

To identify her?

"But couldn't she tell you herself . . . couldn't she declare her name?"

The policemen look at me in bewilderment. The one who's been talking to me until now, but whose words I didn't hear, shrugs and raises his hands in amazement:

"I just explained to you . . . We found her drowned in the river. Last night. It may have been a case of suicide. But we can't exclude it having been an accident, or even murder."

Still quite confused, in spite of the fact that what I'm hearing has shocked me, the words that come to my lips are:

"But what the hell was she doing with my identity card?"

"That's what we asked ourselves," admits the same policeman. "Especially given that it's not an out-of-date identity card, in other words you ought to have reported its loss. When did you last see her?"

"When did I last see *it*, you mean," I hasten to correct the policeman.

"See *what*?"

"The identity card. That's what you mean, isn't it?"

"I was asking you about the woman, not the identity card, sir!"

I smile, slightly amused by the mix-up, then it crosses my mind that this smile isn't appropriate right now, and so, adopting a grave face, I tell them when I last saw my former neighbor. Then, realizing that it's impolite to keep them at the door, I invite them inside.

"And you didn't notice that your identity card was missing?" the other policeman asks, at last, after I have introduced the one in orange suspenders to them as my cousin.

"No, I haven't had time."

When the fuck did she manage to swipe my identity card? And why? I had it on the table. Or on the shelf above the bed. Or in one of the pockets of the trousers I'm wearing now. In fact, I've no idea where my identity card was the day before. And so she could have taken it from anywhere. But why? Did my former lover want to have a photograph of me? In that case, she could have asked me for one. Or did she plan her suicide from the very moment I kicked her out? And she took my identity card to make certain that I'd find out about her death. This last possibility seems the most plausible.

There follows a discussion from which I observe that I'm far from being above the pair's suspicion, but I endeavor to answer their questions as correctly as I can. Even when these prove extremely difficult, lingering on the intimate relationship between my former neighbor and myself.

"Yes, such a relationship did exist," I admit, loyal to the idea of sincerity, "but she ended it yesterday."

"Just like that, all of a sudden?"

"Yes! She didn't like me anymore, and, naturally, we decided it was time for us to go our separate ways."

"Except that her separate way ended up in a river . . ."

The policeman fell silent for a moment, as though impressed by his own profound observation, then he scratches his head, smacks his lips, and adds:

"Are you sure that it was yesterday you split up?"

The policemen look at each other, murmur something among themselves about, as far as I can tell, the end of my intimate relationship with her being a good reason for suicide. Then they stand up and, just as it crosses my mind, in relief, that this'll be the end of it, the one who has spoken asks me to accompany him to the police station.

"Why? Am I under arrest?" I take fright.

I instantly imagine that fate has an irony in store for me, causing me to be arrested for a crime I haven't committed and letting the other one get off scot free.

"No, sir, we just want you to give us a full statement regarding the deceased. You are, according to what you have said, the last person to have seen her alive. Why should we arrest you? Is there any reason we should?" the man in uniform asks, suspiciously.

I vigorously shake my head, as if to say: "No reason at all, mister policeman, sir! I'm a deeply law-abiding man, who has nothing to hide!" And I even force myself to smile, hoping thereby to eliminate any doubt that might be hovering above me. Then I ask them for a few moments so that I can change my clothes.

Chapter Eleven

It's not the first time I've been inside a police station. Leaving aside visits for the purpose of renewing my identity card or passport, there was one occasion when I found myself obliged to spend a number of hours in such a place.

I must have been sixteen or seventeen. And the fact that I ended up at the police station was due to a sect, to a religious cult—the Jehovah's Witnesses, I mean. In fact, it was a result of the interest this cult aroused in me and, above all, the way I deemed fitting to put an end to the connection between myself and the type of God I discovered there.

For a few months I had been frequenting a congregation of Witnesses, I had begun to believe in a part of their theories, I had given up smoking, I wasn't overdoing the booze, and I had even started addressing the other members as "brothers." It was, I must admit, a rather interesting and, above all, not particularly stressful period in my life. That was because back then I was sure of the following: that the Holy Trinity doesn't exist, it's just a stupid fad of the Orthodox; that hell is an invention of the same Orthodox, designed to scare people; that Jesus wasn't crucified on the Cross, as the senile Orthodox likewise claim, but on a wooden post; that the soul and, consequently, ghosts, are just fairy tales, implanted in people's minds by, of course, the same Orthodox; that the Mother of God is nothing more than an offshoot of the cult of the goddess Isis, recklessly adopted by those same cursed Orthodox. In conclusion, it couldn't have been better for me, given that the Witnesses had invented a God completely the opposite of the terrifying God I was used to, a God Who, in effect, chastised a single sin: that of not being a member of the ranks of His beloved faithful, the ranks of Jehovah's Witnesses.

Nevertheless, in spite of the pleasant state into which I had been gradually slipping for a few months, something intervened. A malfunction in the system I had accepted. A malfunction that didn't depend on metaphysical questions, or on misunderstandings, but, quite simply, on my all-too-human nature, all too deeply lacking in the miraculous touch of divinity.

I don't know how, but I let one of the lay friends I still had at the time persuade me to drink a beer with him (the Witnesses didn't forbid alcohol, only drunkenness). Then, slightly tipsy after the first beer, I told myself that God wasn't going to strike me down with a bolt of lightning if I had another. Even tipsier, I reached the conclusion that it would virtually be a sin not to neck another mug, given that the first two had gone down so well. In the end, after I don't know how many beers, judging myself perfectly sober, I decided that it wouldn't be any problem if I drank a little vodka too.

As faith was my main obsession at the time, after I had drunk a bottle of vodka with that friend of mine, I headed off to Kingdom Hall, where the brothers, I had no doubt, would receive me joyously, with flowers and hoorahs. To my stupefaction and that of my companion, however, the brothers looked at me with suspicion, and some of them even invited me to go home. Where, they argued, I would be better off.

The fact that I was being refused, categorically at a given point, communion with God made me feel wronged. All the more so given that—were they really so blind? hadn't they noticed?—I had brought with me a new follower. And I pointed proudly at my friend. Who, in no less good spirits than me, was walking piously among the brothers, kissing them with great love and shouting at the top of his voice:

"Jehovah is the only true God! Long live the great Jehovah! Death to the Orthodox!"

I couldn't understand why such a display of sympathy didn't move the Witnesses to tears, which is why I felt it necessary to accompany the new follower in singing a hymn we knew from childhood. It wasn't until the middle of the hymn that I realized it was, in fact, an Orthodox hymn, given that we were praising from the bottom of our hearts the All-Holy and Immaculate Virgin Mary; but just when I wanted to stop, somehow realizing what a gaffe we had made, two or three of the brawnier Witnesses grabbed our arms and invited us outside.

Of course, such an insult, coming from people I had on countless occasions called "brothers," roused a fury in me which, however hard I tried, I couldn't quell. As a result, I began vigorously flapping my arms and, suddenly recalling the anger that had overcome Jesus in a certain temple, shouting:

"Verily I say unto ye: this house is a house of prayer and you have made it a den of thieves!"

For which reason I no longer cared about anything and, wresting myself from the grip of the brawny Witnesses, the spirit of justice having been awakened in me, I set about demolishing everything around me, seconded in this action by my friend.

I don't know how long the mayhem lasted. All I remember is that, at some point, I began dimly to discern what was happening around me. And I didn't at all like what I could discern. I was in a police station. And next to me, a zealous man in uniform, rhythmically clouting me on the back with a nightstick, was urging me to sign a statement which, he said, I had been reading for half an hour already. In the end, I signed, not so much because I understood what was written on that piece of paper, as much as because the effects of the booze were beginning to fade, and the insistent blows were becoming more and more frequent and, naturally, more painful.

I don't even know how I got out of there. What I do remember very well is that, shortly afterwards, my mother received a summons to present herself at the police station with me, in order to pay a fine. And that was something truly painful. More painful than the pangs of conscience I had had, a few days after the incident, with regard to the Jehovah's Witnesses.

Since then, I have renounced my communion with God. Not only with *that* God. But with any other, be He Orthodox, Catholic, Buddhist or Mohammedan. I didn't negate His existence then, and nor do I definitively negate it now. However, because He insists on presenting Himself to me in such a complex way, in a way so lacking in definite, evident personality, I refuse to waste my time trying to understand Him. I can't see the point. Anyway . . .

Here I am once more obliged to cross the threshold of a police station as a result of a situation which, for the time being, seems less serious in terms of its consequences to my person than the one that took place fifteen or sixteen years ago. But there's no way I can know what's coming next.

∾

After climbing a few steps behind the policemen, they make me wait in a corridor. In front of the door to an office. They point to a chair, on which I seat myself. To my left, standing up, and guarded by another lawman, there's a prisoner—as I can tell from the handcuffs he's wearing. Or to put it more accurately, a six-foot-six giant, who grins enigmatically. And who then winks at me.

I quickly avert my eyes. Because, in spite of the sympathy I feel toward people deprived of their liberty, a sympathy heightened now that there's a theoretical possibility that I too might end up in such a position, I nonetheless prefer not to strike up close relations with any of them.

"Tell me a word," I hear the prisoner's deep voice.

But as I can see no reason why the man should be address-ing me, given that I don't recall ever having met him, I refrain from looking at him. And, staring at the ceiling, I start whistling gently, thereby trying to disguise the nervousness that has over-whelmed me. Then, because there's tension hovering in the air, I start whistling louder. As though the only thing I wished for in life was to sit here, in a corridor of the police station, whistling at the walls.

"Hey, tell me a word!"

This time, however much pleasure it might give me to be mis-taken, I'm almost convinced that he's talking to me. The situa-tion is rather tricky. It's obvious that I can't go on pretending not to notice him. And so I slowly turn my head toward him, putting on an expression that's as surprised as it is innocent.

"Leave the man alone, what do you want with him?" inter-poses the one guarding him, thereby granting me a brief, but intense moment of hope.

Unluckily for me, however, the man in handcuffs doesn't seem very inclined to submit to authority.

"What, aren't I allowed to ask him to tell me a word? What the hell, I'm not hitting him, am I!"

Maybe the guard is also scared. Or maybe the regulations al-low the prisoner to converse with other persons—although, to be honest, I'm quite doubtful about that. What's for sure is that the man in uniform yields and shrugs indifferently, leaving me to cope by myself.

As the giant is looking at me insistently, I give up whistling, realizing that there's no other way to adapt to the situation than to play along with him.

"What word?"

"Any word you like," the one in handcuffs gives me free rein. "But make it a long one."

I think for a few moments of various words, but, as though they too are fearful, they refuse to articulate themselves. In the end, after a few seconds of huge pressure, I manage to blurt:

"Radiator."

"Rotaidar!" promptly comes the giant's reply.

And before the meaning of the prisoner's word can become clear to me, he addresses me again:

"Tell me another, a harder one."

A harder one . . . I don't get it. Would that be a longer one or a more complicated one? I've no idea what he wants from me. To give him some neologisms, or some interminably long words? And, ultimately, what is the point of it all?

Praying that the policemen who brought me here will soon emerge from the office, I try to placate the man on my left, offering him both possibilities in a single word:

"Circumvolution!"

"Niot-ulov-mucric. What kind of a nasty word is that, *circumvolution*?" he asks, visibly annoyed.

"A word like any other," I shrug, allowing myself to act clever.

"Like any other—that's what *you* think! Didn't you see how hard it was for me to pronounce it backwards?"

At last, I have every reason to breathe a sigh of relief! His mumblings were nothing more than the words I told him, but pronounced backwards! I don't know how, but the giant to the left of me suddenly becomes likeable.

The man guarding him titters like a child, then points at the prisoner, gleefully:

"That's the first time you haven't been able to say a word backwards all in one breath. You have to admit, he won that time."

"What do you mean *won*?" the one in handcuffs snaps back at him, angered. "You mean to say that was a word? I never heard such a word in my life! It was something foreign. I've never boasted that I can reverse words from another language!"

"Oh, come off it," the warder smiles condescendingly, "stop trying to make excuses . . . He won and that's the end of it!"

While the two of them are arguing amiably, giving each other amused nudges from time to time, I, although I've no idea how exactly I won, begin to feel better and better. And so I get ready to utter some even more difficult words.

Unfortunately, however, I'm not given the chance. One of the two men in uniform who brought me here pokes his head through the office door and invites me inside.

I go into the office, thoroughly well disposed. Though I probably shouldn't feel this way. Above all, I ought not to appear like this in front of suspicious policemen. Bearing in mind the fact that I'm here to give a statement about a deceased person. With whom, moreover, I've also had intimate relations. But I'm not thinking about any of that now. I'm thinking about the two left behind in the corridor who thanks to their attitude have made me change my opinion about life in prison. If all prison inmates were like that, and, perhaps more importantly, if all guards were like that, I probably wouldn't object to admitting that it was I who killed the prostitute in the bar. At confessing that I killed her, even if she's in perfect health right now. Ultimately, I would only stand to gain. A strict timetable, meals served at set times, and, as a bonus, relaxing conversations with the guards or fellow inmates. Moreover, I would no longer have the window ledge to lure me, to offer me room to wait for a suicidal urge.

Penitentiary. Pen-i-ten-ti-ary. "Yra-ti . . . No, damn it! Yra-it-net-i-nep," my mind strives to arrange the word backwards, while a policeman, not the one I already know, holds out a pen and a sheet of paper.

I write the statement with a wealth of details, even adding, without anyone asking, intimate details when I reach the paragraph describing my relationship with my former neighbor. And, the closer I get to the end of the statement, more and more images from the time I spent with her take shape in my mind. And together with these images, I become aware that the woman I had the chance to know so well is now dead. That she died by committing suicide. That is, by doing something I have long been intending to do, but without success. I even realize, as I write the final paragraph, in which I relate how our final meeting unfolded, that I'm touched by a slight regret. Then, more surprisingly even than the regret, I'm overwhelmed by a wave of admiration. She is—she was—the only person I know who really has managed to kill herself!

For the first time, I think that, had I paid more attention to my former neighbor, I could have come to love her. And this observation curtails the pleasant state in which the previous conversation left me, inducing nostalgia, with my former neighbor in the leading role.

After I sign the piece of paper, the policemen advise me not to leave town until the investigation has been concluded. Then they allow me to go.

In the corridor, the prisoner who succeeded, to a certain extent, in changing my image of prison, asks me to put him to the test one more time.

"Intramuscular," I say without enthusiasm, remembering the word I had prepared for him before going into the office.

Then, no longer having any curiosity to check whether he manages to say it backwards correctly, I bid him farewell, leave the corridor of the police station and head for home.

Chapter Twelve

On a child's first birthday, the parents, almost without exception, conform to tradition and place before their progeny a platter full of various objects. If they have a boy, it's almost obligatory to lay on the tray the following: a pop gun, a remote-controlled car, a battery-powered airplane, a toy pickaxe or spade, a screwdriver, even a packet of cigarettes or a pipe. If they have a girl, then it's other, specifically feminine things: a lipstick, a little handbag, a few necklaces, a bobbin of thread, a dinner plate . . . Regardless of the child's sex, on that platter will also be placed, on top of all the other objects if necessary, a crayon and a drawing book. Once all these have been placed before the progeny, the parents wait impatiently for the birthday boy (girl) to choose one of them. If the boy chooses the pickaxe, the father, bursting with pride, will exclaim:

"We'll make a structural engineer of him!"

It would never even cross his mind to imagine his child, in the future, becoming a laborer, wielding a pickaxe.

If he chooses the airplane, likewise bursting with joy, the same father will exclaim:

"Daddy's little aviator!"

Would it even cross his mind that his progeny might end up working in some airport ticket office?

If the pistol attracts the child, the masculine voice will give the following verdict, with just as much joy:

"Oh, ho, ho, Mr. Police Inspector!"

What else but an inspector? A gangster, perchance?

Or the girl: lets suppose she chooses the lipstick.

"A supermodel," the mother will cry, "our daughter is going to be a supermodel!"

In no case a temperamental slut!

The bobbin of thread:

"A famous fashion designer, no doubt about it!"

A lowly seamstress, eking out a meager living?

But nothing could bring greater joy to the parents than if the child chooses the exercise book or the pencil. They won't get "scientist" or "writer" out of their heads for a long time.

Supposing by some absurd chance I ever had children, I'd probably place something entirely different on the first-year-birthday platter. A noose made of thin rope. A phial of cyanide. A syringe for drugs. A knife. A pistol, even if I thereby lapse into the banal. And many other similar things. If I truly thought that this tradition provided a clue about fate, I'd in this way be able to discover what kind of death awaited my child. Or, in the case in which he chose nothing from the tray, I'd know that he wasn't cut out to be a suicide . . .

The wide-open door to my flat interrupts these not particularly intelligent thoughts. Could my friend with the orange suspenders be airing the room? I think not. There would be no need. The window is almost constantly open. What then? Might I have been robbed?

I step, in great agitation, over the threshold. The man who's been my guest for the last couple of days is nowhere in the flat. At first glance, none of my most important possessions are missing. As I don't have any jewels hidden in a back drawer, as I don't keep any money in a safe, as valuable paintings have never adorned my walls, apart from the television and, possibly, a few clothes in the cupboard there's nothing here for a burglar to steal. Moreover, even the clothes in which I dressed my friend, for his short career as a postman, are folded on the bed. Which makes me conclude that he's left my home without being forced by anyone or anything. And without leaving me any explanation.

However, in order to find out from reliable sources what exactly has happened, I go out of my flat and ring at the door of my neighbors opposite, the door which is always ajar between the hours of six in the morning and six in the evening. No sooner do I ring than the old man pokes his head through the crack and says, cantankerously:

"I've already been to see the superintendent, you know, young man. I don't care what relative of yours that vagabond is.

He can be your cousin, brother, son, son-in-law, for all I care. What is important is that he's staying in your apartment, having his meals in your apartment, sleeping in your apartment, and so I've notified the superintendent. Why should you pay communal bills for just one person when there are two people living there?"

These words ought to annoy me. But I show no reaction. I don't see why I should react, given that I can expect no other kind of reception on his part.

"Let's leave that to one side," I make a conciliatory gesture with my hand. "Did you see him at the moment he left?"

"Leave it to one side, young man?" the old man barks. "Do you really think it can be passed over so easily? All the people in this block are honest when it comes to paying their bills, but you want to defraud the state? What, are you telling me that that vagabond didn't consume any water?"

"And methane gas!" can be heard, from behind the door, the voice of my interlocutor's consort. "Don't forget the methane gas."

"Yes, and methane gas! Both water and gas!"

"He didn't even wash all the time he was staying with me," I smile.

"I could see that by the way he looked. Filthy from head to toe. But didn't he drink any water?"

I shrug, realizing there's not much I can answer to such a question.

"Let him pay for the water he drank!" the old man won't let it lie. "We're not going to pay, all the people in this block, for him!"

Then, after a pause:

"Yes, I saw him leave."

Overjoyed that he has, at last, got to what I am interested in, I ask:

"And?"

"And . . . what?" the old man doesn't understand my question.

To be honest, not even I very well understand what exactly I want to find out from my neighbor.

"If you want to find out more, then let me inform you that he was whistling when he left, young man! Do you hear? He was whistling on the landing of a block where there are old people! Why doesn't the sinner go and whistle in a church? Old people need peace and quiet, you know. After a life of toil, they have a right to rest. Not like you young people today, who don't work and live off others' backs . . ."

My arms crossed, a grimace of boredom in the corner of my mouth, I nonetheless nod in agreement, hoping that the old man will get his apologia for his generation over with more quickly, the generation that went through so many adverse times, the generation that knew the meaning of forced collectivization and futile waiting for help to come from the Americans, the generation that buried its brothers slain in the mountains because they dared to name themselves partisans, the generation that . . .

And when you think that I have to listen to all this just because my friend with the orange suspenders dared to drink a few glasses of the communal water!

When, at last, my neighbor deems that he's made me understand a part of life's truths, he pauses for a moment, breathing heavily, and adds:

"And another thing, young man, your guest left the door open. Do you realize what could have happened? If I wasn't here to guard your door, you wouldn't have had a thing left in the house now!"

I offer him a "thanks" that is bored and sneering at the same time, after which I go to my own flat. Before closing the door, I hear my neighbor say:

"And take out your garbage, young man, because it smells. It's not enough that you keep your garbage pail full to the brim—you had to fill two plastic bags as well! And wash the sink, if you don't want the place to be overrun with maggots!"

The fact that he wasn't content merely to guard the flat, but also thought it his duty to make an inspection of the inside ought, once again, to anger me. It ought to, but not even this time does this happen.

∽

If it were evening, I'd go straight to the locomotive that serves as a dwelling place for my friend with the orange suspenders. In the evening, I'm almost convinced, he'll be there. But it's barely midday, and so it's hard for me to imagine where he might be now. Maybe in some bar. Maybe roaming the streets at random. Maybe . . .

Although there are not many chances of finding him until evening, I have to get out of the house. Here, it wouldn't be long until I got back to thinking black thoughts about my future behind bars. Albeit a life behind bars now appears to me in a gentler light, after the discussion I had with the prisoner in the hall of the police station.

What's for sure is that I have to get out of the house. There's nothing for me to do here. The pornographic magazines no longer attract me, especially in the present situation. Even the thought of them, combined with the memory of the recent death of my former neighbor, makes me feel guilty, as though I would be tainting something sacred, as though I were a blasphemer. And there's no point climbing onto the window ledge; there are too many people down below and I'd be embarrassed.

I have to get out of the house. However, just as I'm about to do so, I hear the doorbell. The superintendent of the block in which I live, the breeder of cats whose husband died of heart disease fifteen years ago, is smiling benevolently at me in the doorway, waiting for me to invite her inside.

∾

Today is a day of neighbors. After the irritating, but at the same time, I must admit, rather amusing discussion with the one opposite, it's now the turn of the superintendent to offer me a few minutes of her life. Or rather to take up a few minutes of mine. In order for my day to be complete, I'd probably have to listen, over a cigarette, to my neighbor with the jam-jar-bottom spectacles telling the story of how his first wife cheated on him with a doctor, of how he went off to war and broke his leg falling into a trench, of how they put him down as wounded in action, of how he returned home to find his second wife with a doctor, of how, furious, he applied for medical school so that he could be a doctor too, of how he didn't get in because he had just been afflicted by an eye disease, and of how he wanted to be a surgeon, and of how, because of this, he now has such a small pension . . . Yes. The only thing this day lacks would be an encounter with my neighbor who wears the extraordinarily thick jam-jar-bottom glasses.

Just as benevolent, the superintendent sits in the armchair I point to.

"I've come to tell you," she finally says, "that I haven't taken any notice of the backbiting of those malcontents opposite, and I haven't put you down as two persons on the list for maintenance charges."

"All right, thank you," I say, determined to get rid of this woman as quickly as possible.

"Would you be a nice boy and make me a cup of coffee?" she shatters my hope, smiling amiably.

I can't refrain:

"Why?"

If she could understand the meaning of this question, as it exists for me, the woman in my armchair would have to answer to the following: "Why do you all keep driving me mad with your wretched lives, why do you live here, in the same block as me, why don't you all throw yourselves headfirst out of your windows, you cranky old men, you old biddies still scarred by menopause, you over-the-hill women with pickled lips painted bright red? And, ultimately, why the hell were you born at all?" However, given that my "why?" merely sounds banally irritable, she, scolding me gently, can only answer:

"Well, isn't that the nice way to treat your guests?"

Guests . . . I curse her in my mind for the serene smile she's displaying and for the wish she's expressed. However, in the end, I put the kettle on, reckoning that I don't really have many excuses to kick her out.

While we're drinking our coffee, she tells me in great detail about how my neighbors from opposite came to her, about how they explained to her, with the utmost outrage, that in our block a new person had been living for a number of weeks, about how . . .

"He's been staying with me for just two days," I interrupt her at this point in the story. "In fact, not even two whole days have passed."

"Exactly what I thought too! They're faultfinders, people without scruples. All they do is sling mud at people who, unlike them, are very nice! Very nice!"

Pleased with the compliment, inasmuch as it is obvious that I am included in the category of the "very nice," I go on listening to her, with somewhat more goodwill than up to now.

A curious thing then happens. As she continues to express her indignation at the behavior of some of the people who live in our block, I notice her wink her right eye a few times insistently. And I don't really know how to interpret this: as a nervous tic she can't shake off or a means of conveying to me a certain complicity, born of the already acknowledged liking she has toward me? However, I don't know her well enough to find an answer to this dilemma. In any case, her gesture would have a certain charm, if she were ten years younger.

"Have you heard," she asks, after taking another sip of coffee and relinquishing her indignation, "what happened to the former fireman?"

I shrug and twist my lips in ignorance.

"Ah, well then, I'll tell you."

I sigh. And I get ready to listen.

"He went out of the building, with his white cane. You know his white cane, don't you?"

"Yes . . ."

"Anyway," she goes on, after receiving my affirmative answer, "he went out with his cane, pretending that he was blind, and he had his marmalade money in his pocket. But, as luck would have it, he wasn't to know that a kid would try to steal his money. Well, that's just what happened: a kid, one of those urchins, who live on the street or down in the manholes, tried to steal his money. Feeling the kid's hand in his pocket, our neighbor lost his temper and, ha, ha, can you imagine how stupid, he forgot to pretend he was blind. He started chasing the little thief down the street, shouting, and, in the end, he threw his cane at him. He didn't catch him, of course, but that's not important. Well, what do you think happened next?"

I shrug once more, bored.

"You're not going to believe this: he was seen by one of the people who think he's blind. Since then, ha, ha, the former fireman isn't allowed to go to the front of the line because the one who saw him told everyone about what happened."

She's looking at me, expecting me to be enthused at hearing of such an event, but I, however hard I might try to be amiable, can only say, dully:

"Interesting."

Because she doesn't see me laughing, the superintendent then wipes the smile off her face, sighing affectedly. Then, for a short time, an awkward silence settles between us.

"How is our former tenant, who moved to the country?" she enquires eventually, putting on a different kind of smile, one full of implied meanings.

"Well . . ."

"I heard from the same neighbors who came to me with the complaint—as you can see, they're shameless gossipers too—that you had an argument yesterday and . . . Well, I'll tell you: she's supposed to have left your flat in tears."

It doesn't surprise me that she knows about all this. It's natural for the two snoopers, who permanently keep their door ajar, to know in minute detail everything that happens on our landing. For this reason I'm convinced that in fact the woman in front of me would have liked to ask: "How is your former lover?" Because it's easy to deduce that she's no stranger to the whole story of my amorous liaison. The only thing that amazes me is that she doesn't know about the visit from the police. Could the spies opposite have been asleep at the time?

How is my former lover? I could tell her she's dead. Moreover, if I insisted at all costs on creating an aura of absolute masculinity for myself, I could admit that she killed herself because of me. But I can't be bothered with that right now. And so, of course, I shrug for the third time.

"I understand that you like mature, experienced women," the superintendent adds somewhat playfully and again winks her right eye.

This time, almost beyond any doubt, I find the explanation for her gesture. She doesn't have a tic. She's merely trying to re-gather the shadows of the coquettish feminine charm she once possessed, in order to . . . This woman, who is smiling so pleasantly at me and insistently winking at me, is trying to flirt with me!

My conclusion is also borne out by the foot which, under the coffee table that separates us, is zealously caressing mine.

"Please don't get me wrong, but . . . Sometimes, for nice people, I can give discounts on maintenance bills. It can be done, if you know how to do the sums," she is trying, red-faced, to make me as attractive an offer as possible, still laughably moving her legs so as to touch me. "Now, if you've broken up with her anyway, I assume you're single, aren't you?"

I abruptly stand up, moving slightly further away, avoiding the legs stretched out under the table. And as she, visibly embarrassed, resumes a dignified posture, it's my turn to smile. I must admit: it would have been quite hard for me to expect something like this. What the hell! How could I have expected it? I don't even know whether up until today, apart from on official matters, I've exchanged more than twenty words with the superintendent!

I look closely at the woman in front of me. In spite of a few wrinkles, of the heavily rouged lips, of the thinning hair, she doesn't seem wholly unattractive to me. If she had been ten years younger . . . I think that it's too difficult to make a decision on the spot regarding her, especially taking into account the events that have turned my life upside down in the past three days. And so, still smiling, I tell her:

"A discount on maintenance bills wouldn't come amiss. The problem is that it's not yet the case for us to talk about that. You see, today I have a few problems to . . . We can talk about it another day."

Her blush visibly deepens, and her face lights up. The promise she senses in my words even makes her quiver slightly.

"Are you sure we can talk about it?" she asks, almost imploringly.

I nod, affirmatively. Then I take advantage of the newly established closeness between us and explain, without standing on ceremony, that I have to go out somewhere. She gets up from the sofa and, as happy as can be, extends her hand to me.

I watch her enter the elevator; she's sprightly, as though rejuvenated by the ten years that would be required to make her attractive. Then, left alone, as always after such moments, I begin to laugh.

Chapter Thirteen

I'll never understand what it is that pushes me into situations I'm powerless to resolve. Some would jump up and cry at the top of their voice: "Fate, that's what!" Fate, my ass! God? Him, maybe. Him, yes. In my opinion, the opinion of a man who's long since given up idolatrizing God, He endowed us with free will merely for His own amusement. There's no way He could have amused Himself with a bunch of marionettes. Only children play with dolls, endowing them with life in their own imagination. But He knows all too well the difference between imagination and reality. And so He gave us free will and thereby set Himself up with a whole host of gags. We, down here, monkey around, while He laughs. He sits comfortably in the best seat in the house, His angels are all comfy in the stalls, and we, the comedians, are up there on stage. Now and then, He guffaws or, depending on how we perform, gets annoyed. When He laughs, He applauds us and gives us the feeling that we've pulled His leg. When He gets irritated at one of us, He sneers with the all-too-common curse: "The devil take you!"

But I don't think it's the case for me to be philosophizing about God. I haven't done this for a long while. Because I don't see any point in it. In any case, the wise words that the Deity has sent for the benefit of mankind have never been of any use to me. Or, perhaps . . . Perhaps once. They were of use in bringing me closer to my brother, for whom, up until then, I'd never had much of a liking. Nor he for me.

My brother had from an early age shown signs that between him and the One Above there was a special relationship. He's the only one in our family who had ever managed to swoon in church while the choir was intoning "Hosanna," when he was about three years old. Well, I had always had my doubts about the emotion that overwhelmed my brother at that age, putting his swoon down to the suffocating incense smoke in church. But neither my mother nor my grandmother was of my opinion. They always upheld that the child's swoon wasn't due to worldly causes, but rather represented the moment in which he was brushed by an angel's wing. From that moment, in the family of which I was part the future of the boy two years younger than me was meticulously laid out. And I was constantly forced to put up with being compared to him. Comparisons which, naturally, could hardly not bother me.

My mother and grandmother impatiently waited for the years to pass. An impatience heightened by the fact that, at their insistence, my brother had finished reading the Bible when he was about ten, had learned by heart a whole host of passages from the *Psalter* by the age of twelve, had read with much zeal *The Lives of the Church Fathers* when he was about thirteen and, finally, in the year when he was to sit the entrance exams for the Theological Seminary, at the age of fourteen, he had read passages from *The Russian Pilgrim* in the church in my grand-parents' village. And the peasant women had wept and caressed his head and said that yes, the angel had given him his blessing. So, anyone can imagine how many tears were shed and how many thrashings he endured when, two months before the examination, my brother said he was giving up the Theological Seminary.

"But not my faith," he assured the family, "no, good people, not my faith. I believe in God more than ever. But, you see, not in the false God in Whom you believe," he added.

And this word *you* was uttered with scorn, with as much scorn as a child of fourteen with a squeaky but determined voice, can put in his words.

"And who, pray tell, is the new God you believe in?" I asked him the following night, looking at the bruises left by the spruce switches that grandmother, red in the face, foaming at the mouth in fury, had ripped from the tree behind the shed.

"The only true God," came the squeaky and determined voice from under the same quilt, a voice somehow altered by sighs. "The One who is not denatured by traditions and other fabrications of the human mind. I believe in Jehovah."

"Since when?"

"For a long time. For a few months, but I haven't had the courage to tell anyone up until now."

To my great surprise, bearing in mind the relationship between us, I took pity on my young brother then and embraced him. Maybe I too wept a little there, in bed, next to him, then I patted him on the head and told him something which, bearing in mind I was sixteen years old and had few antecedents in the field of faith, proved to be an extraordinarily mature remark:

"You know, some people are offered a God, others find Him for themselves. The important thing is that only those people who come across God like that, off their own back, can boast that, look, they have discovered the Lord Above. The others can't do that, because He's given to them on a plate, they haven't got the brains to seek Him."

After that came the only teaching of God to mankind which, as I argued, had been of any use to me.

"A while back you yourself used to say that in the Bible it is written: 'Seek me, and ye shall find' . . ."

My brother lit up then, I can almost swear that I saw his face illumined in the darkness of the room, and he told me he loved me, because I was right. I told him I loved him and I embraced him once more. I felt clever and deep then, although, I must admit, I was a bit surprised that he hadn't remembered the divine words that had come into my head.

From that moment, my brother and I became the best of friends. All the more so because he repeated that he loved me many times, and I continued to urge him Socratically to know himself and, in this way, to find the true God. What's more, out of love for my brother, in a short time I then became interested in the God Whom I was advocating to him. And so I ended up going, for a few months, to meetings of the Jehovah's Witnesses.

In the meantime, my brother discovered—the same as me, except for different reasons—that neither was Jehovah quite true. And, in revenge at the God Who forbade men to bear arms, he became an officer in the army. Since then, since he became a respectable man, he has refused to acknowledge me as his brother, because I, who had been expelled from university on the grounds of repeated drunkenness, was nothing but a lowlife, the dregs of society, a man of whom no one could be proud.

But I don't know what came over me just now, thinking about my brother, about all those things that compel me to be melancholic. However, it's important to keep my mind occupied with something to chase away the images of life behind bars that are haunting me even now that I have left the building.

∾

Something doesn't add up. Why am I so afraid of prison? Everything could be solved simply: when the investigation about the prostitute (in the unhappy case that she's dead) led to my friend with the orange suspenders and, implicitly, to me, I would have a means of escape. I'd climb, as I have been doing for so long, onto the window ledge. And, in such a situation, the urge would have to come. It's logical: there'd be no way it couldn't come! Ultimately, up until now my desire to commit suicide has been an attempt to cancel out tomorrow. An attempt to cancel out any possible future. I don't know why I have been seeing my future so clearly of late, when, in principle, I have the option of death. I don't understand why my prisoner's pajamas are already starting to chafe. I don't know why prison bars have turned into such an obsession for me. Something, without doubt, doesn't add up.

Maybe I have too many wishes. Maybe this is why the urge doesn't come. Do I really have so many and such strong wishes? If I do, what are they? For a beautiful woman to look after me and have sex with me until I feel my heart giving out? To inherit money from some hypothetical uncle in America? To be a footballer and to play, if only for five minutes, in the most famous stadium in Italy? To be elected president? To invent a device, like a magnet, that will attract all the money lost by all the people in the world? These are idiocies, not wishes.

What then is the cause of my fear of prison? I have always been convinced that I would throw myself out of the window without hesitation if I felt the urge. But the problem here might be whether some silly idea has slipped into my unconscious which says that in fact it would be better for the urge in question never to come. Whether this unconscious of mine is, like an idiot, going by hopes, by images of something better, refusing to see that nothing, ever, anywhere, has any point. In the case in which this were true, all my mornings spent on the window ledge would be transformed into tawdry buffoonery. And the only thing that would remain for me to do would to be a sad, a terribly sad, man who lacks even the elementary courage to end his life in a dignified fashion. But, of course, this isn't true!

A possessor of desires that hindered suicide was sooner that old acquaintance of mine who desired a dog's death.

"I'd round a few stray dogs up," he used to say. "I'd put them in a sack, and go into the woods. Then I'd hang them all from a tree. I'd hang myself, next to those dying dogs. So that the whole world would understand what kind of life I've had and see what kind of death fell to my lot."

"What kind of death?"

Apart from the cruelty with which he wanted to hang some poor dogs, nothing could make me find anything extraordinary in such a death. But I, it would seem, couldn't understand metaphors as well as he could.

"What, don't you get it? After a dog's life, a dog's death!" he explained.

Although it all sounded like cheap melodrama, if he had put his idea into practice, I would have considered it, in the end, estimable. However after repeatedly describing in all its gory details the moment he saw as glorious, just as he was on the point of arousing my respect and maybe even admiration, he announced that he was getting married. I haven't seen him since.

Yes, that acquaintance of mine might be accused of desires. The proof also resides in the fact that he fulfilled one of them, that of getting married, giving up the thought of suicide. Whereas I . . . What might I be accused of? Perhaps only of desiring—why don't I admit it?—to have sex with the superintendent of the block in which I live. But that desire was born only a short time ago, only a few hours ago. Whereas the fear of prison I've been feeling for many, many more hours. Since it never even crossed my mind to imagine the superintendent harboring a passion for me. In other words, since there were no desires to place an obstacle in the way of suicide.

Since, in spite of my efforts, I can't manage to reach any other conclusion, I conclude that once again I have willfully tangled myself up in riddles that have no chance of being unraveled. Dissatisfied, I accept the observation: "Something doesn't add up, nonetheless," then I chase away all these wearying thoughts, trying to discern which part of the city my feet have led me to.

~

I go over to the fountain in the city's main square and sit down on a bench. The clouds have already acquired vesperal outlines, while my mind was occupied with thoughts that led to no conclusion. What's more, I have covered a considerable distance on foot, as far as the center of the city, and so it's natural to feel the need to rest for a few minutes.

On my left, two old men are shaking dice in their hands and casting them onto a backgammon board. Above me, some pigeons are fluttering their wings, flying close to the ground, in tight circles, presaging rain. "No doubt about it," I look up at the overcast sky, "it will rain tonight."

Down below, near the bench on which I'm sitting, a beggar, who can't be more than fifteen or sixteen, is dragging his stump legs along on a trolley made from a piece of wood, to which he has attached some rollers. He comes up to my legs and looks at me, smiling inanely, exposing crooked teeth. I smile too, because I've got nothing else to do. I smile, he smiles. Or rather, I am grinning in puzzlement; he is grinning from hunger, probably. Or from . . . How should I know from what?

"What do you want?" I ask him finally.

He goes on grinning, without making any move, as though he hasn't heard the question.

"Tell me what the hell you want!" I raise my voice, already irritated by the situation.

"A cigarette," the other's voice comes to me at last, somewhere from the depths of a cavity guarded by crooked teeth.

"What do you need it for?" I ask sagely, as if a cigarette might be used in any number of different ways.

"Because I need one, that's why," the man at my feet continues to bare his teeth to me.

"What will you do for a cigarette?"

I don't even know what I meant by that. What am I expecting from him? To make funny faces, to clap his hands, to grunt like a pig, to do all kinds of clownish tricks for a cigarette? I remember my thoughts about God and I realize that I'm demanding gags from the beggar, as though in some kind of revenge against the One Above. Probably so as to make Him understand that at this moment I'm like Him, controlling the life (or at least a moment in the life) of a poor wretch. How stupid!

"I'll sing you a carol," says the one at my feet. "Or . . ."

Just at the moment when, conscious of the stupid way in which I'm trying to spite the One Above, I'm on the point of giving the cripple a cigarette without demanding anything in return, the words he adds manage to stir a certain interest in me.

"Or, if you like, I'll tell you about a cousin of mine who's in Italy."

To sing a carol to get something in return, even if Christmas is still quite a way off, seems appropriate for a beggar. But to tell me about some cousin or other in Italy? I've never heard that one before.

"Tell me about that cousin of yours," I say, putting the cigarette back in the packet.

The one at my feet notices how close he was to getting a cigarette without further pretensions on my part, and he regrets having let his words carry him away, as is plain from his face. And so, given that he no longer has anything to lose anyway, he raises the stakes:

"But will you give me some money too?"

"No. I haven't got any money. But I'll give you three or, look, even five cigarettes. All right?"

The one on the trolley nods his head, only half satisfied, then, sighing as though he were preparing himself for some tedious task, he starts to tell the story:

"I have a cousin in Italy. And he has some pigeons, the ones that take letters where you tell them to go. He says in the pigeon's ear: 'Hey, pigeon, off you go to where I'm sending you!' And off the pigeon goes, poor thing, he's got no choice. My cousin sends letters to us, to the whole family, like that. With them pigeons. And not just letters, if you must know. All kinds! Except once, the pigeons got caught by the mafia over there. Do you what the mafia is?"

"The mafia, of course, I know."

He takes no notice of me.

"They're real bad ones," he nonetheless sees fit to explain to me. "And because they're bad ones, after they caught them pigeons, those mafia bandits cut the wings off the poor pigeons."

He stops, still grinning at me. And I, even though I'm not so gullible as to imagine that the one at my feet really has a cousin in Italy, and even though I'm sure that he heard this story somewhere and adopted it for the purposes of making money, have to admit that this is an original way of begging. And I want to see where it all will lead. But the toothy grin has frozen on his face, and he shows no intention of continuing.

"So?" I ask. "Is that all? That's the story?"

He shakes his head. Then he stretches out his hand.

"First you give me a cigarette, then I'll tell you the end."

"No, because then you'll run off."

"I won't run off, honest! What, do you think I'm faster than you with your two legs?"

I realize that, from his trolley, even the word "run" must seem completely meaningless. And so I pull five cigarettes from the packet, then I place them one by one in his outstretched palm. He thrusts them in his pocket and goes on:

"There's not much more to tell. Just that the pigeons got here in the end with the letters. You know how? The poor things came all that way on foot!"

I look at the beggar in astonishment, but I don't manage to get a word in as regards the tall tale he's just told, because he starts propelling himself along the asphalt with his hands, and the trolley carries him away. Probably in search of another mark desirous to hear his tale about the Italian mafia.

$\sim$

I walk along the railway tracks of the marshalling yard, remembering that, forty-eight hours ago, I was in the same place, heading toward the station. Then, all I desired was to find a prostitute (and I found one; but unfortunately, just when I met her, she got a chair broken over her head). Now I'm hoping to find my friend with the orange suspenders. And at this hour there's no better place to seek him than in the locomotive he's made his home.

I don't even know why I so much want to meet him again. Perhaps because I'm curious to find out whether, in the meantime, he's found out what happened to the girl he hit in the bar. And, proceeding from there, perhaps because I'm afraid. I'm afraid he might have killed himself, in the case in which the girl didn't survive . . .

Together with this fear, I understand, almost in self-disgust, why images of life behind bars have been haunting me lately. Because, regardless of whether the prostitute is dead or not, I'm now almost certain of one thing: the urge is never going to come, however long I wait for it on the window ledge! And so it's not about him, about my friend with the orange suspenders, that I'm worried. But rather—damn it all!—about myself. If the girl is dead, and if he's managed to kill himself (which is highly likely, given that not long ago he himself said: "If she'd kicked the bucket, I wouldn't have hesitated to kill myself; I wouldn't have fooled around, I wouldn't have hoped someone would save me, I'd have killed myself, and that would've been that"), I'll be on my own, like a fool, waiting every day for the police to come knocking at my door. Of course, with all those desires stocked in my unconscious. With all those idiotic desires, which I refuse to acknowledge, but which put a damper on my impulse.

Having almost reached the locomotive, I look closely at its sides. The two pieces of rail are in their place. But I have cause to breathe a sigh of relief: there's no noose attached to them.

And so, as there remains nothing for me to do outside, I climb the steps to the former engine-driver's cabin, hoping from the bottom of my soul to find my friend with the orange suspenders here.

Chapter Fourteen

To my relief, he's in the cabin.

He turns toward me, giving a slight start, at the moment I appear in the doorway. Then, recognizing me, he puts his hand on his chest, breathes a sigh of relief and, finally, greets me, giving me a wave. A greeting that simultaneously expresses revulsion and goodwill, as though he'd been expecting me to come, but, at the same time, would have been happy for his expectations not to have been borne out.

"How are you?" I ask stupidly, not having any other ideas as to how to start the conversation.

"All right," he answers mechanically, just as stupidly, but forced by my question.

The next moment we stand in silence, looking at one another, without finding any way to continue the conversation. However, the fact that I notice him hiding something behind his back succeeds in breaking the moment of silence, just in time.

"What have you got there?"

"Nothing."

"You're hiding something behind your back. What do you mean, nothing?"

"Like I said, nothing."

This exchange, which stifles any trace of intelligence, continues. Which irritates me, especially given that, in this way, our conversation has every chance of being peppered with lengthy silences, for which I don't really understand the reason. What the hell? What could be the justification for the tension between us?

"You went off leaving the door open!" I snap, determined to provoke him into speaking nonetheless. "What if thieves had stolen my stuff?"

"What stuff?" he grins at me. "You haven't got much more stuff than me," he goes on, making a sweeping gesture with his hands, showing me the locomotive cabin he's made his home. "And I'm not at all scared to leave the door open."

Not that he'd have anything to close, for the simple reason that, from what I can observe casting a fleeting glance, the locomotive doesn't have a door. If it had doors once, and it would have been absurd for it not to, they have been taken off their hinges and probably sold for scrap. As for the interior . . . Even if the coal dust, mixed with all kinds of oil, has left a black, greasy layer on the walls, I can say about this room, a former engine-driver's cabin, that it's not very far removed from my idea of comfort. Over what was once the dashboard my friend with the orange suspenders has thrown a piece of canvas painted with little flowers, probably once more colorful than the grey it is now, which stretches over a surface of about six feet in length and one and a half feet in width. On this surface, in a corner, almost touching the window, there stands a potted plant, without any trace of flowers, filled with earth. The plant is wrapped in tinfoil. In the middle, in an earthenware jug with a broken lip, are thrust a spoon and two knives. Finally, on the side opposite the plant pot, there's an old gas lamp. With a bit of imagination, I might think this surface were meant to be a table. On the floor, next to what has already been accepted to be a table, there are two cooking pots, rusted on the outside, and a box full of folded-up clothes. Also on the floor, less than three feet away from the box of clothes, is a bed. A bed? Sort of . . . Fenced in by the obvious traces of two rails (so this is what my friend uses the two pieces of iron for, apart from in his suicide attempts: to mark out the space where he sleeps), it passes as a bed because of a pillow, also greasy, and two sheets carefully folded up in one of its corners.

This is more or less a complete picture of the interior of the locomotive-dwelling. If I think that, besides the things my friend has, all I possess is a television, a nightstand, two armchairs and a genuine bed, then I'm almost in agreement with my friend's opinion about the thieves who wouldn't have had much to steal from my apartment. And if I add to all this the fact that here he doesn't pay rent or maintenance bills, it would probably not take much to make me feel a certain envy.

"Yes. You've fixed the place up nicely," I say, nodding in appreciation.

He answers flatly:

"Yes, I have."

And this attitude, which maintains the tense atmosphere, makes me think it's highly likely that he's found out something about the prostitute in the bar (can he have found out—God forbid!—that she's dead?). And that, by coming here, I'm disturbing him in a very important matter: that of committing suicide. He all but confirms my suspicion when he says:

"I'd have liked you to come later."

"Why?" I raise my voice. "So that you would have had time to kill yourself?"

He looks at me like a dimwit, and the surprise he displays seems sincere.

"Why would I kill myself? Now that you've told me she didn't kick the bucket, now that I've got nothing to worry about, why would I kill myself?"

He gives me a look from which I ought to understand that I've cheered him up with my stupid suspicions. Kill himself! Would you listen to that! As if he hadn't got anything better to do!

And this certainty of his manages to cheer me up too. Because it all becomes very clear to me: I was frightened for no reason. Even if he were guilty of murder, not even he would be capable of killing himself, the same as I'm not. He wouldn't be capable of doing anything except what he's been doing up to now: staging a suicide, taking a number of risks, it's true, but hoping at the same time, from the bottom of his soul, that someone would save him. And hoping that, in the end, he'd be forgiven for his crime. All his attempts to kill himself, it's clear to me, were nothing but the vainglory of a weak man (a man just as weak as I am, let me not be unjust). Nevertheless, in spite of certain principles I thought I had, this observation doesn't bring with it any contempt toward my friend with the orange suspenders.

"That's why I'd have liked you to come later," he holds out two pieces of twine, which he's been hiding behind his back. "I was just about to make them into nooses when you came in."

I just don't get it! A few seconds ago he seemed outraged by my suspicion, and now he's showing me these two pieces of twine . . . Can the madman want us to commit suicide together? Was my whole previous conclusion about his weakness wrong? Does he really want to kill himself?

The confusion doesn't last more than a few seconds. His cheerful face, the way he's fluttering the two nooses beneath my eyes, makes me understand. "If we pretend to kill ourselves," he told me this morning, "the railway workers will think we're sorry for all that stuff that happened in the bar. That we're sorry about beating up the prostitute and that we didn't want to kill her. And maybe like that, they'll forgive us."

It still seems as though I'm the only one who has to suffer. I'm the only one still wracked by uncertainty. My friend with the orange suspenders has once more become the one whom the nurse at the dispensary told me about, the one tormented by a single thought: "What can I do to be forgiven?" In other words, what can he do to go on living in his railway station, to come back to his locomotive without a care, to spend his nights in his bar, drinking his glass of vodka on the slate? Reduced to the essentials: what the hell can he do to go on living his life in his own way?

"What do you say?" he asks, impatiently twirling those nooses in his hand. "Shall we do it?"

All my previous conclusions about the man in front of me make me have a feeling of regret. And make me smile, under the impulse of a plan that begins to take shape in my mind. Make me smile and shrug, as if to say: "What else can we do?"

∿

After the efforts we put into repositioning the pieces of rail and securing them as rigidly as possible inside the cabin, we allow ourselves a few minutes to rest.

I go out and look from in front of the locomotive, so as to get as broad a view as possible. The two long pieces of iron give the locomotive a grotesque air, like a huge bird, with skeletal wings eroded by the wind. The moments in which I admire this image are cut short, however. My friend asks me to test the resistance of the gallows intended for me, the one situated above the entrance to the right of the locomotive. After which he tests his, above the other entrance, gripping the rope with his hands and letting his body dangle in the air. The rope holds, the rail likewise.

At last, satisfied with the job done, we sit down, each next to his noose, waiting in the dark for some railway worker to pass.

"It has to be a railway worker," he explains, "because that way the news about us"—and sticking out his tongue raises his hand and makes a gesture as though he were yanking a rope—"will reach the ones who were in the bar three evenings ago. If some guy from town saves us we'll not have solved anything. So that they'll feel sorry for us and forgive us for that brawl, it has to be a railway worker who finds us."

This wait, irritating for me, but rather satisfying for him it would seem, to judge by the expression I can glimpse on his face, is going on far too long. As I don't see why I should wait in silence for some railway worker to come, I permit myself to speak, trying to satisfy my curiosity:

"Tell me, given that you've never intended to die, why the fuck do you position the noose so far from the locomotive? That way, when you let yourself drop, there's no chance of you catching hold of the locomotive and saving yourself. Wouldn't it be more convenient to place it closer, so that you could save yourself if need be?"

He shakes his head, as a sign that this question is proof of my amateurism as regards suicide or, in any case, a well-organized, fake suicide, and he explains:

"If I did that and someone realized that I could get out of the noose by myself, all this toil would go to hell. As soon as he understood that I was trying to fool him, the news would get out, and that would be the end of it. Who would believe me after that?"

"Does anyone believe you anyway? That nurse at the dispensary knew that you didn't want to kill yourself for real."

The fact that I remind him of this visibly rankles him. He gesticulates, muttering something to himself, then explains:

"Yes, she knew. I told her, once, and since then she keeps asking me all kinds of questions. I had no choice. I was almost a goner when I told her, I didn't know what I was doing. It was after the train accident I had."

"Train accident?"

I recall the nurse's story once again. She told me something about this. What's more, she said something about two such suicide attempts.

"Aha," my friend answers. "That was before I found the rails. The first time, when I put my head on the track, some guys pulled me clear of the oncoming express at the last moment. The second time, I don't know what the hell happened. I was lying with my neck on the track, the train was coming, and I was waiting calmly to be yanked by the coat and pulled out of the way, like the first time. Except just at the moment when some railway workers wanted to pull me away, I got caught, I don't know how the hell, and fell right on my face between the lines. Lucky I had that padded coat on. Now, you know, every locomotive has one of those guards, and so that guard caught my coat and instead of the train passing over me it dragged me along. What can I say? I survived! Anyway, after that I was cured of trains . . ."

He breaks off his story, putting his hand to his ear to listen.

"Sssh . . ."

I prick up my ears too, peering ahead, trying to make out what it is he seems to hear. Within a few seconds I too become certain that someone is coming our way.

"See whether he's a railway worker," he whispers from my left.

I try to glimpse in the dim lights of the station whether the man is wearing a uniform. I can't make it out. But it seems that my friend with the orange suspenders has keener vision, because he says to me, in the same low voice:

"He's got a hard hat on, he's a railway worker. Except . . ." He hesitates a few seconds, looks very closely, then: "Except he's no good."

"Why the hell wouldn't he be any good?" I whisper, annoyed.

I just don't get it. What's my friend waiting for? For the man approaching to have a qualification in the field of suicide? To produce his rescuer-of-mad-suicides-who-hang-themselves-from-locomotives certificate before we entrust ourselves into his hands?

"Sssh . . ."

The man is drawing ever closer. My friend signals me to sit in the area he considers his bed, so as to be hidden from the eyes of the approaching man. He sits down too. We sit in silence, tensed, until we hear his footsteps passing by the locomotive and then receding into the distance. At last, although still keeping my voice down, I repeat the question:

"Why the hell wasn't he any good?"

"He just wasn't . . ."

He's not even looking at me. He goes out of the door and, shielding his eyes with his hand, as though there were a blinding light, he looks down the railway tracks.

"Wasn't it one of the ones who were in the bar?"

"No," he says, still with his back turned to me, "it wasn't one of those . . ."

"How the hell could you tell? It's dark. What, do you know them all so well that . . ."

"Yes, I know them."

"Like hell you know them! Tell me: why wasn't he any good?"

He turns toward me at last. It seems to me he's hiding something. Then he tries to say something but stops. He waves his hand and resumes his previous position, gazing toward the station.

"What's up with you? What don't you want to tell me?"

"Nothing."

"Well, I can see that you don't want to tell me anything. But I don't know why! What kind of secret are you keeping from me?"

He gives up looking outside. He sits down on the greasy pillow and asks me for a cigarette. He lights it and puffs on it as he looks somewhere over the cabin dashboard, over the table, in other words. I watch the smoke, which curls somewhere over the potted plant wrapped in tin foil, then drifts toward the window over the dashboard, forming . . . Enough. Enough!

"Why didn't that railway worker suit you?" I raise my voice. "What was wrong with him? Was he a leper or what?"

"Can't we talk about something else? You'd think you were a nagging old woman: what was wrong with that railway worker, what was wrong with that railway worker" he mimics me. "I didn't like his face, that's what! You can leave yourself in the hands of whoever you like, but it doesn't suit me to be saved by someone whose face I don't like!"

"You're mad!"

He looks at me abruptly, raising his forefinger:

"I'm not mad!"

"Then why . . ."

"I'm not mad!" he emphasizes, almost threateningly.

"All right, man, you're not."

In the end, I don't even understand myself. Maybe he truly didn't like that man's face. Or maybe he was the one who he'd had the fight with and he knew he wouldn't save him. Who knows? Why should I wrack my brains with such questions? Maybe my insistence on finding out is caused by the plan I have hatched. I want it to be over already. I want to . . .

He suddenly stands up and rushes to the place where the locomotive's door ought to have been. In the following moment, I realize why he's stood up. A whistle can be heard somewhere far off. My friend is looking with concentration at the man who's approaching. Without turning around toward me, he makes a sign for me to stand up.

"This one's good," I hear him say eventually.

Then he urges me to put the noose around my neck, and I conform. I'm holding onto the bar which long ago used to aid the mechanic to climb into the cabin, and I'm shivering. The noose I can feel around my neck heightens my tension. I turn my head toward my friend. Holding onto the bar, he's leaning his body outwards, waiting for the moment when the railway worker will draw close enough. He too is shivering.

"Now!" I finally hear.

I see him drop in the noose. And so, finally rid of my nervousness, I take the noose from my neck, according to the plan I had hatched earlier. Then I quickly climb down the steps, trying to hide myself from the eyes of the man who's approaching along the railway tracks, whistling. Unfortunately, just as I start running away behind the locomotive, I get the stupid idea of looking one more time at the railway worker. And I stop running, cursing with all my heart the man, who, unexpectedly, changes direction, moving away toward . . . the devil knows where! Thwarting my plan. And annoying the hell out of me.

I want to keep on running, not to care, to leave my friend with the orange suspenders in the hands of fate. To leave him there, hanging in the noose. For a few paces, I even succumb to the temptation. But in the end, I curse once more the moron who saw fit to change direction all of a sudden, just when everything seemed to be going according to plan. And I go back.

The railway worker is walking away from the locomotive, heading toward a building somewhere on the right. If I were paranoid, I'd think his change of direction was premeditated. But I'm not. That's why I realize the man hasn't seen my friend hanging in the noose; I realize that it was all down to chance. But this is precisely what makes me even more furious.

Because there's no way I can control my temper and because he's receding placidly, whistling without a care, I lay my hand on a stone and toss it in his direction. He stops.

"I threw it!" I scream at him, waving my hands in the air, to make sure he sees me. "Got a problem with that?"

In spite of my anger I notice that this question isn't born of any gleam of my intelligence. But this common-sense observation doesn't prevent me from laying my hand on another rock and hurling it in the direction of the railway worker.

He jumps to one side to avoid it.

"What the fuck do you want?" I hear his voice at last.

"For you to fucking die, that's what I want!" I howl, angry that not even with the second stone did I hit my target. "For you to croak!"

The man, after a few seconds of hesitation, decides to make a run for it. And I can find nothing else to do except run after him. And, as I run, to keep grabbing stones. And throwing them in his direction. Nor do I forget to curse with all my heart. This chase soon ends, however. Because after a given point the railway worker, fresher than I am, vanishes from my field of vision. Which provides me with a respite to remember my friend with the orange suspenders.

I curse once, furiously, then run back, panting, to the locomotive. I get the hanged man down from the noose, I lay him on the ground, I slap him twice. Then I slap him some more. However, because he doesn't seem too bothered by my slaps, and makes no movement to show he might still be alive, I tell myself that I will have to try a different treatment.

And while I am giving him mouth-to-mouth resuscitation, the image of my former neighbor comes into my mind. Who, nodding her head understandingly, says to us: "Don't be ashamed, darlings; my husband, God forgive him, used to say to me too: 'If it weren't for you, woman, I really don't know what I'd do; I'd probably bat for the other side.'"

At last, my friend with the orange suspenders begins to cough, setting me at ease. After a few moments, he looks around him in bewilderment . . . At last, he holds onto my arm, and pulls himself up into a sitting position. Then he asks me, amid fits of coughing:

"What the hell happened?"

I wave my hand in disgust.

"Nothing," I say.

He seems irritated by my reply, but doesn't dwell on it. We're sitting like this: I, on my bottom, on the stones between the tracks, with my hands on my hips, devoid of thoughts; he, holding onto my arm, still coughing, choked by the air to which his lungs are only just becoming re-accustomed.

After a while, my attention turns to the two long pieces of rail which lend the locomotive its odd look, that of a huge bird with skeletal wings eroded by the wind. And once again I'm struck by the awareness of an incongruity, the same as when I saw the horse in my cousin's dining room, the same as when I saw the expensive whiskey in my pal the former theologian's pail. The incongruity between thin, useless wings and this black, iron structure, huge in comparison with them.

Without understanding why, I feel a need to confess to the one beside me:

"I don't know if that prostitute is alive or dead."

He surprises me with a guffaw, or rather a guttural rattle that resembles a roar of laughter.

"You know," he says. "Don't make out that you don't know. I . . . I know too. I found out. Did you imagine that I'd . . . that I'd believe you, just like that, just because you said so?"

Even more surprised, I wait for him to go on. He doesn't, however.

"And?" I ask, at last. "Did she survive?"

My friend, choking, coughing, struggling to draw as much air into his lungs as he can, is nonetheless unable to quell his laughter:

"That railway worker . . . the railway worker was carrying a toolbox, didn't you notice? That's why I said that the first . . . the first wasn't any good; the first didn't have any tools, he was coming straight toward us . . . he was going to the marshalling yard, he works in the marshalling yard. He didn't have tools . . . He passed right by us, as you saw yourself. But the other one . . . Didn't you realize? He wasn't coming toward the locomotive, he was going to the depot . . . only the ones that work in the depot have that toolbox . . . it was obvious . . . I realized as soon as I saw him. The depot . . . the depot is on that side," he points his hand in the direction where the man I threw the stones at had run away.

"Then," I say in revolt, "if you knew he wasn't heading toward us, if you knew he wouldn't save us, why the hell did you hang yourself? Why did you make me put my head in the . . ."

All of a sudden, I realize there's no point continuing the question, because the answer is simple. He knew what had happened to the prostitute, he knew that that railway worker was never going to save us, he knew that we would both hang, in our nooses, until the day pigs fly. He knew that I would die too, alongside him, like a simpleton, without needing any urge, any window ledge, any reason or any lack of a reason. He knew. And this is what he would have wanted to happen. And it wasn't hard to make the connection. Not at all hard.

"And you say you found out what happened to her," I say, in a calm, resigned voice.

"Yes. That's why I came here: to find out. You were too scared when those policemen showed up at the door. I thought to myself that you have your reasons to be scared."

"Yes," I agree, "I was scared. But I didn't know at the time. I didn't manage to find out anything when I was at the station, yesterday evening. I didn't tell you, because I felt pity at how you were torturing yourself merely at the thought you might have . . ."

My friend with the orange suspenders says nothing else. He sits, stooped, with his head in his hands, struggling to draw air into his chest.

"And are you sure? She's really dead?"

He raises his head from his hands and nods to show that he has no doubt. The swollen eyes, his distraught eyes fixed on me, the wide-open mouth, the slightly protruding tongue, the quivering chin . . . This image, one wholly inappropriate to the moment, swells my chest with a roar of laughter.

A few moments later, in the nocturnal silence of this marshalling yard, all that can be heard are our guffaws. Mine, drawn-out, an outburst for which, were there a need, I could find no explanation. His, an accompanying guffaw, tortured, halting, broken by repeated fits of coughing.

LUCIAN DAN TEODOROVICI is the senior editor of *Suplimentul de cultură*, one of the most prominent weekly cultural magazines in Romania. He has contributed prose, drama, and nonfiction to magazines in Romania and abroad, and has written numerous screenplays, including one for a feature-length adaptation of *Our Circus Presents* . . . .

ALISTAIR IAN BLYTH's translations from Romanian include the novel *Little Fingers* by Filip Florian and *An Intellectual History of Cannibalism* by Cătălin Avramescu.

SELECTED DALKEY ARCHIVE PAPERBACKS

PETROS ABATZOGLOU, *What Does Mrs. Freeman Want?*
MICHAL AJVAZ, *The Other City.*
PIERRE ALBERT-BIROT, *Grabinoulor.*
YUZ ALESHKOVSKY, *Kangaroo.*
FELIPE ALFAU, *Chromos.*
    Locos.
IVAN ÂNGELO, *The Celebration.*
    The Tower of Glass.
DAVID ANTIN, *Talking.*
ANTÓNIO LOBO ANTUNES, *Knowledge of Hell.*
ALAIN ARIAS-MISSON, *Theatre of Incest.*
JOHN ASHBERY AND JAMES SCHUYLER, *A Nest of Ninnies.*
HEIMRAD BÄCKER, *transcript.*
DJUNA BARNES, *Ladies Almanack.*
    Ryder.
JOHN BARTH, *LETTERS.*
    Sabbatical.
DONALD BARTHELME, *The King.*
    Paradise.
SVETISLAV BASARA, *Chinese Letter.*
MARK BINELLI, *Sacco and Vanzetti Must Die!*
ANDREI BITOV, *Pushkin House.*
LOUIS PAUL BOON, *Chapel Road.*
    My Little War.
    Summer in Termuren.
ROGER BOYLAN, *Killoyle.*
IGNÁCIO DE LOYOLA BRANDÃO, *Anonymous Celebrity.*
    Teeth under the Sun.
    Zero.
BONNIE BREMSER, *Troia: Mexican Memoirs.*
CHRISTINE BROOKE-ROSE, *Amalgamemnon.*
BRIGID BROPHY, *In Transit.*
MEREDITH BROSNAN, *Mr. Dynamite.*
GERALD L. BRUNS, *Modern Poetry and
    the Idea of Language.*
EVGENY BUNIMOVICH AND J. KATES, EDS.,
    Contemporary Russian Poetry: An Anthology.
GABRIELLE BURTON, *Heartbreak Hotel.*
MICHEL BUTOR, *Degrees.*
    Mobile.
    Portrait of the Artist as a Young Ape.
G. CABRERA INFANTE, *Infante's Inferno.*
    Three Trapped Tigers.
JULIETA CAMPOS, *The Fear of Losing Eurydice.*
ANNE CARSON, *Eros the Bittersweet.*
CAMILO JOSÉ CELA, *Christ versus Arizona.*
    The Family of Pascual Duarte.
    The Hive.
LOUIS-FERDINAND CÉLINE, *Castle to Castle.*
    Conversations with Professor Y.
    London Bridge.
    Normance.
    North.
    Rigadoon.
HUGO CHARTERIS, *The Tide Is Right.*
JEROME CHARYN, *The Tar Baby.*
MARC CHOLODENKO, *Mordechai Schamz.*
EMILY HOLMES COLEMAN, *The Shutter of Snow.*
ROBERT COOVER, *A Night at the Movies.*
STANLEY CRAWFORD, *Log of the S.S. The Mrs Unguentine.*
    Some Instructions to My Wife.
ROBERT CREELEY, *Collected Prose.*
RENÉ CREVEL, *Putting My Foot in It.*
RALPH CUSACK, *Cadenza.*
SUSAN DAITCH, *L.C.*
    Storytown.
NICHOLAS DELBANCO, *The Count of Concord.*
NIGEL DENNIS, *Cards of Identity.*
PETER DIMOCK, *A Short Rhetoric for Leaving the Family.*
ARIEL DORFMAN, *Konfidenz.*
COLEMAN DOWELL, *The Houses of Children.*
    Island People.
    Too Much Flesh and Jabez.
ARKADII DRAGOMOSHCHENKO, *Dust.*
RIKKI DUCORNET, *The Complete Butcher's Tales.*
    The Fountains of Neptune.
    The Jade Cabinet.
    The One Marvelous Thing.
    Phosphor in Dreamland.
    The Stain.
    The Word "Desire."
WILLIAM EASTLAKE, *The Bamboo Bed.*
    Castle Keep.
    Lyric of the Circle Heart.
JEAN ECHENOZ, *Chopin's Move.*
STANLEY ELKIN, *A Bad Man.*
    Boswell: A Modern Comedy.
    Criers and Kibitzers, Kibitzers and Criers.
    The Dick Gibson Show.
    The Franchiser.
    George Mills.
    The Living End.
    The MacGuffin.
    The Magic Kingdom.
    Mrs. Ted Bliss.
    The Rabbi of Lud.
    Van Gogh's Room at Arles.
ANNIE ERNAUX, *Cleaned Out.*
LAUREN FAIRBANKS, *Muzzle Thyself.*
    Sister Carrie.
JUAN FILLOY, *Op Oloop.*
LESLIE A. FIEDLER, *Love and Death in the American Novel.*

GUSTAVE FLAUBERT, *Bouvard and Pécuchet.*
KASS FLEISHER, *Talking out of School.*
FORD MADOX FORD, *The March of Literature.*
JON FOSSE, *Melancholy.*
MAX FRISCH, *I'm Not Stiller.*
    Man in the Holocene.
CARLOS FUENTES, *Christopher Unborn.*
    Distant Relations.
    Terra Nostra.
    Where the Air Is Clear.
JANICE GALLOWAY, *Foreign Parts.*
    The Trick Is to Keep Breathing.
WILLIAM H. GASS, *Cartesian Sonata and Other Novellas.*
    Finding a Form.
    A Temple of Texts.
    The Tunnel.
    Willie Masters' Lonesome Wife.
GÉRARD GAVARRY, *Hoplla! 1 2 3.*
ETIENNE GILSON, *The Arts of the Beautiful.*
    Forms and Substances in the Arts.
C. S. GISCOMBE, *Giscome Road.*
    Here.
    Prairie Style.
DOUGLAS GLOVER, *Bad News of the Heart.*
    The Enamoured Knight.
WITOLD GOMBROWICZ, *A Kind of Testament.*
KAREN ELIZABETH GORDON, *The Red Shoes.*
GEORGI GOSPODINOV, *Natural Novel.*
JUAN GOYTISOLO, *Count Julian.*
    Juan the Landless.
    Makbara.
    Marks of Identity.
PATRICK GRAINVILLE, *The Cave of Heaven.*
HENRY GREEN, *Back.*
    Blindness.
    Concluding.
    Doting.
    Nothing.
JIŘÍ GRUŠA, *The Questionnaire.*
GABRIEL GUDDING, *Rhode Island Notebook.*
JOHN HAWKES, *Whistlejacket.*
ALEKSANDAR HEMON, ED., *Best European Fiction 2010.*
AIDAN HIGGINS, *A Bestiary.*
    Balcony of Europe.
    Bornholm Night-Ferry.
    Darkling Plain: Texts for the Air.
    Flotsam and Jetsam.
    Langrishe, Go Down.
    Scenes from a Receding Past.
    Windy Arbours.
ALDOUS HUXLEY, *Antic Hay.*
    Crome Yellow.
    Point Counter Point.
    Those Barren Leaves.
    Time Must Have a Stop.
MIKHAIL IOSSEL AND JEFF PARKER, EDS., *Amerika:
    Russian Writers View the United States.*
GERT JONKE, *Geometric Regional Novel.*
    Homage to Czerny.
    The System of Vienna.
JACQUES JOUET, *Mountain R.*
    Savage.
CHARLES JULIET, *Conversations with Samuel Beckett and
    Bram van Velde.*
MIEKO KANAI, *The Word Book.*
HUGH KENNER, *The Counterfeiters.*
    Flaubert, Joyce and Beckett: The Stoic Comedians.
    Joyce's Voices.
DANILO KIŠ, *Garden, Ashes.*
    A Tomb for Boris Davidovich.
ANITA KONKKA, *A Fool's Paradise.*
GEORGE KONRÁD, *The City Builder.*
TADEUSZ KONWICKI, *A Minor Apocalypse.*
    The Polish Complex.
MENIS KOUMANDAREAS, *Koula.*
ELAINE KRAF, *The Princess of 72nd Street.*
JIM KRUSOE, *Iceland.*
EWA KURYLUK, *Century 21.*
ERIC LAURRENT, *Do Not Touch.*
VIOLETTE LEDUC, *La Bâtarde.*
SUZANNE JILL LEVINE, *The Subversive Scribe:
    Translating Latin American Fiction.*
DEBORAH LEVY, *Billy and Girl.*
    Pillow Talk in Europe and Other Places.
JOSÉ LEZAMA LIMA, *Paradiso.*
ROSA LIKSOM, *Dark Paradise.*
OSMAN LINS, *Avalovara.*
    The Queen of the Prisons of Greece.
ALF MAC LOCHLAINN, *The Corpus in the Library.*
    Out of Focus.
RON LOEWINSOHN, *Magnetic Field(s).*
BRIAN LYNCH, *The Winner of Sorrow.*
D. KEITH MANO, *Take Five.*
MICHELINE AHARONIAN MARCOM, *The Mirror in the Well.*
BEN MARCUS, *The Age of Wire and String.*
WALLACE MARKFIELD, *Teitlebaum's Window.*
    To an Early Grave.
DAVID MARKSON, *Reader's Block.*
    Springer's Progress.
    Wittgenstein's Mistress.
CAROLE MASO, *AVA.*

FOR A FULL LIST OF PUBLICATIONS, VISIT:
www.dalkeyarchive.com

SELECTED DALKEY ARCHIVE PAPERBACKS

LADISLAV MATEJKA AND KRYSTYNA POMORSKA, EDS.,
Readings in Russian Poetics: Formalist and
Structuralist Views.
HARRY MATHEWS,
The Case of the Persevering Maltese: Collected Essays.
Cigarettes.
The Conversions.
The Human Country: New and Collected Stories.
The Journalist.
My Life in CIA.
Singular Pleasures.
The Sinking of the Odradek Stadium.
Tlooth.
20 Lines a Day.
ROBERT L. MCLAUGHLIN, ED., Innovations: An Anthology of
Modern & Contemporary Fiction.
HERMAN MELVILLE, The Confidence-Man.
AMANDA MICHALOPOULOU, I'd Like.
STEVEN MILLHAUSER, The Barnum Museum.
In the Penny Arcade.
RALPH J. MILLS, JR., Essays on Poetry.
MOMUS, The Book of Jokes.
CHRISTINE MONTALBETTI, Western.
OLIVE MOORE, Spleen.
NICHOLAS MOSLEY, Accident.
Assassins.
Catastrophe Practice.
Children of Darkness and Light.
Experience and Religion.
God's Hazard.
The Hesperides Tree.
Hopeful Monsters.
Imago Bird.
Impossible Object.
Inventing God.
Judith.
Look at the Dark.
Natalie Natalia.
Paradoxes of Peace.
Serpent.
Time at War.
The Uses of Slime Mould: Essays of Four Decades.
WARREN MOTTE,
Fables of the Novel: French Fiction since 1990.
Fiction Now: The French Novel in the 21st Century.
Oulipo: A Primer of Potential Literature.
YVES NAVARRE, Our Share of Time.
Sweet Tooth.
DOROTHY NELSON, In Night's City.
Tar and Feathers.
WILFRIDO D. NOLLEDO, But for the Lovers.
FLANN O'BRIEN, At Swim-Two-Birds.
At War.
The Best of Myles.
The Dalkey Archive.
Further Cuttings.
The Hard Life.
The Poor Mouth.
The Third Policeman.
CLAUDE OLLIER, The Mise-en-Scène.
PATRIK OUŘEDNÍK, Europeana.
FERNANDO DEL PASO, News from the Empire.
Palinuro of Mexico.
ROBERT PINGET, The Inquisitory.
Mahu or The Material.
Trio.
MANUEL PUIG, Betrayed by Rita Hayworth.
Heartbreak Tango.
RAYMOND QUENEAU, The Last Days.
Odile.
Pierrot Mon Ami.
Saint Glinglin.
ANN QUIN, Berg.
Passages.
Three.
Tripticks.
ISHMAEL REED, The Free-Lance Pallbearers.
The Last Days of Louisiana Red.
The Plays.
Reckless Eyeballing.
The Terrible Threes.
The Terrible Twos.
Yellow Back Radio Broke-Down.
JEAN RICARDOU, Place Names.
RAINER MARIA RILKE,
The Notebooks of Malte Laurids Brigge.
JULIÁN RÍOS, Larva: A Midsummer Night's Babel.
Poundemonium.
AUGUSTO ROA BASTOS, I the Supreme.
OLIVIER ROLIN, Hotel Crystal.
JACQUES ROUBAUD, The Form of a City Changes Faster,
Alas, Than the Human Heart.
The Great Fire of London.
Hortense in Exile.
Hortense Is Abducted.
The Loop.
The Plurality of Worlds of Lewis.
The Princess Hoppy.
Some Thing Black.
LEON S. ROUDIEZ, French Fiction Revisited.

VEDRANA RUDAN, Night.
STIG SÆTERBAKKEN, Siamese.
LYDIE SALVAYRE, The Company of Ghosts.
Everyday Life.
The Lecture.
Portrait of the Writer as a Domesticated Animal.
The Power of Flies.
LUIS RAFAEL SÁNCHEZ, Macho Camacho's Beat.
SEVERO SARDUY, Cobra & Maitreya.
NATHALIE SARRAUTE, Do You Hear Them?
Martereau.
The Planetarium.
ARNO SCHMIDT, Collected Stories.
Nobodaddy's Children.
CHRISTINE SCHUTT, Nightwork.
GAIL SCOTT, My Paris.
DAMION SEARLS, What We Were Doing and
Where We Were Going.
JUNE AKERS SEESE,
Is This What Other Women Feel Too?
What Waiting Really Means.
BERNARD SHARE, Inish.
Transit.
AURELIE SHEEHAN, Jack Kerouac Is Pregnant.
VIKTOR SHKLOVSKY, Knight's Move.
A Sentimental Journey: Memoirs 1917–1922.
Energy of Delusion: A Book on Plot.
Literature and Cinematography.
Theory of Prose.
Third Factory.
Zoo, or Letters Not about Love.
JOSEF ŠKVORECKÝ, The Engineer of Human Souls.
CLAUDE SIMON, The Invitation.
GILBERT SORRENTINO, Aberration of Starlight.
Blue Pastoral.
Crystal Vision.
Imaginative Qualities of Actual Things.
Mulligan Stew.
Pack of Lies.
Red the Fiend.
The Sky Changes.
Something Said.
Splendide-Hôtel.
Steelwork.
Under the Shadow.
W. M. SPACKMAN, The Complete Fiction.
ANDRZEJ STASIUK, Fado.
GERTRUDE STEIN, Lucy Church Amiably.
The Making of Americans.
A Novel of Thank You.
PIOTR SZEWC, Annihilation.
GONÇALO M. TAVARES, Jerusalem.
LUCIAN DAN TEODOROVICI, Our Circus Presents . . .
STEFAN THEMERSON, Hobson's Island.
The Mystery of the Sardine.
Tom Harris.
JEAN-PHILIPPE TOUSSAINT, The Bathroom.
Camera.
Monsieur.
Running Away.
Television.
DUMITRU TSEPENEAG, Pigeon Post.
The Necessary Marriage.
Vain Art of the Fugue.
ESTHER TUSQUETS, Stranded.
DUBRAVKA UGRESIC, Lend Me Your Character.
Thank You for Not Reading.
MATI UNT, Brecht at Night
Diary of a Blood Donor.
Things in the Night.
ÁLVARO URIBE AND OLIVIA SEARS, EDS.,
The Best of Contemporary Mexican Fiction.
ELOY URROZ, The Obstacles.
LUISA VALENZUELA, He Who Searches.
PAUL VERHAEGHEN, Omega Minor.
MARJA-LIISA VARTIO, The Parson's Widow.
BORIS VIAN, Heartsnatcher.
ORNELA VORPSI, The Country Where No One Ever Dies.
AUSTRYN WAINHOUSE, Hedyphagetica.
PAUL WEST, Words for a Deaf Daughter & Gala.
CURTIS WHITE, America's Magic Mountain.
The Idea of Home.
Memories of My Father Watching TV.
Monstrous Possibility: An Invitation to
Literary Politics.
Requiem.
DIANE WILLIAMS, Excitability: Selected Stories.
Romancer Erector.
DOUGLAS WOOLF, Wall to Wall.
Ya! & John-Juan.
JAY WRIGHT, Polynomials and Pollen.
The Presentable Art of Reading Absence.
PHILIP WYLIE, Generation of Vipers.
MARGUERITE YOUNG, Angel in the Forest.
Miss MacIntosh, My Darling.
REYOUNG, Unbabbling.
ZORAN ŽIVKOVIĆ, Hidden Camera.
LOUIS ZUKOFSKY, Collected Fiction.
SCOTT ZWIREN, God Head.

FOR A FULL LIST OF PUBLICATIONS, VISIT:
www.dalkeyarchive.com